TWELFTH NIGHT; OR, WHAT YOU WILL

William Shakespeare

DOVER PUBLICATIONS, INC.
MINEOLA, NEW YORK

DOVER THRIFT EDITIONS

Copyright

Theatrical Rights

Bibliographical Note

This Dover edition, first published in 1996, contains the unabridged text of *Twelfth Night; or, What You Will* as published in Volume VI of *The Caxton Edition of the Complete Works of William Shakespeare*, Caxton Publishing Company, London, n.d. The Note was prepared specially for this edition, and explanatory footnotes from the Caxton edition have been supplemented and revised.

Library of Congress Cataloging-in-Publication Data

Shakespeare, William, 1564–1616.
   [Twelfth night]
   Twelfth night, or, What you will / William Shakespeare ; [edited by Candace Ward].
      p.   cm. — (Dover thrift editions)
   "Contains the unabridged text . . . as published in Volume VI of The Caxton Edition of the Complete Works of William Shakespeare . . . explanatory footnotes from the Caxton edition have been supplemented and revised"—T.p. verso.
   ISBN-13: 978-0-486-29290-8 (pbk.)
   ISBN-10: 0-486-29290-8 (pbk.)
   I. Ward, Candace. II. Title. III. Series.
PR2837.A2W27   1996
822.3'3—dc20   96-38467

                                    CIP

Manufactured in the United States by LSC Communications
29290816   2020
www.doverpublications.com

Note

TWELFTH NIGHT (C. 1600–1601) is one of Shakespeare's most joyful plays, bringing together in a grand mixture many of the stock elements of comedy. Here may be found the maiden disguised as a man, the twins separated by mischance, the lovelorn suitor and the puritanical buffoon—all characters loaded with comic potential. The very choice of *Twelfth Night* as a title reveals the play's festive nature, alluding to the Feast of the Epiphany (January 6), the last day of the revelry-filled Christmas season. Traditionally a time when plays were performed, banquets and masques were held and some release was to be had from rigid morality, it was also a time to celebrate joy and to lampoon those (such as the play's Malvolio) who would curb gaiety and dampen merriment. In keeping with this spirit, *Twelfth Night* closes amidst a carnival atmosphere, with all disguises cast off and all trickery revealed, with the siblings reunited and the killjoy brought down, and with the promise of three weddings to be celebrated.

The first recorded performance of the play was on February 2, 1602, although some scholars believe that it had already been staged on Twelfth Night of the year before (hence its name). As a source, Shakespeare was probably most influenced by one of the stories in Barnabe Riche's *Riche his Farewell to Militarie profession* (1581), which in turn took many of its plot elements from earlier French and Italian works. Whereas *Twelfth Night* casts a kind eye upon frivolity and abandon, however, Riche's story has a moralizing tone, blaming its characters' carnal appetites for the difficulties they encounter. It may well be that Shakespeare intended the disapproving Malvolio to be a parody of the censorious Riche, for the story of his comeuppance is unique to Shakespeare's version of the tale. It was a memorable addition, and popular: so much so that for many years the play was known solely by the title *Malvolio*.

Contents

Dramatis Personæ

ORSINO, Duke of Illyria.
SEBASTIAN, brother to Viola.
ANTONIO, a sea captain, friend to Sebastian.
A Sea Captain, friend to Viola.
VALENTINE,
CURIO, } gentlemen attending on the Duke.
SIR TOBY BELCH, uncle to Olivia.
SIR ANDREW AGUECHEEK.
MALVOLIO, steward to Olivia.
FABIAN,
FESTE, a Clown, } servants to Olivia.

OLIVIA.
VIOLA.
MARIA, Olivia's woman.

Lords, Priests, Sailors, Officers, Musicians, and other Attendants.

SCENE: *A city in Illyria, and the sea-coast near it*

ACT I

SCENE I. *An apartment in the* DUKE'S *palace.*

Enter DUKE, CURIO, *and other* Lords; Musicians *attending*

DUKE. If music be the food of love, play on;
    Give me excess of it, that, surfeiting,
    The appetite may sicken, and so die.
    That strain again! it had a dying fall:
    O, it came o'er my ear like the sweet sound,
    That breathes upon a bank of violets,
    Stealing and giving odour!
    Enough; no more:
    'T is not so sweet now as it was before.
    O spirit of love, how quick and fresh art thou!
    That, notwithstanding thy capacity
    Receiveth as the sea, nought enters there,
    Of what validity and pitch soe'er,
    But falls into abatement and low price,
    Even in a minute! so full of shapes is fancy,
    That it alone is high fantastical.
CUR. Will you go hunt, my lord?
DUKE.   What, Curio?
CUR. The hart.
DUKE. Why, so I do, the noblest that I have:
    O, when mine eyes did see Olivia first,
    Methought she purged the air of pestilence!
    That instant was I turn'd into a hart;
    And my desires, like fell and cruel hounds,
    E'er since pursue me.

Enter VALENTINE

                How now! what news from her?

1

VAL.   So please my lord, I might not be admitted;
    But from her handmaid do return this answer:
    The element[1] itself, till seven years' heat,
    Shall not behold her face at ample view;
    But, like a cloistress, she will veiled walk
    And water once a day her chamber round
    With eye-offending brine: all this to season
    A brother's dead love, which she would keep fresh
    And lasting in her sad remembrance.
DUKE. O, she that hath a heart of that fine frame
    To pay this debt of love but to a brother,
    How will she love, when the rich golden shaft
    Hath kill'd the flock of all affections else
    That live in her; when liver, brain and heart,
    These sovereign thrones, are all supplied, and fill'd
    Her sweet perfections with one self king!
    Away before me to sweet beds of flowers:
    Love-thoughts lie rich when canopied with bowers.   [*Exeunt.*]

SCENE II. *The sea-coast.*

Enter VIOLA, *a* Captain, *and* Sailors

VIO.   What country, friends, is this?
CAP.   This is Illyria, lady.
VIO.   And what should I do in Illyria?
    My brother he is in Elysium.
    Perchance he is not drown'd: what think you, sailors?
CAP.   It is perchance that you yourself were saved.
VIO.   O my poor brother! and so perchance may he be.
CAP.   True, madam: and, to comfort you with chance,
    Assure yourself, after our ship did split,
    When you and those poor number saved with you
    Hung on our driving boat, I saw your brother,
    Most provident in peril, bind himself,

---

1. *element*] sky.

Courage and hope both teaching him the practice,
To a strong mast that lived upon the sea;
Where, like Arion on the dolphin's back,
I saw him hold acquaintance with the waves
So long as I could see.

VIO.   For saying so, there 's gold:
Mine own escape unfoldeth to my hope,
Whereto thy speech serves for authority,
The like of him. Know'st thou this country?

CAP.   Ay, madam, well; for I was bred and born
Not three hours' travel from this very place.

VIO.   Who governs here?

CAP.   A noble Duke,[1] in nature as in name.

VIO.   What is his name?

CAP.   Orsino.

VIO.   Orsino! I have heard my father name him:
He was a bachelor then.

CAP.   And so is now, or was so very late;
For but a month ago I went from hence,
And then 't was fresh in murmur,—as, you know,
What great ones do the less will prattle of,—
That he did seek the love of fair Olivia.

VIO.   What 's she?

CAP.   A virtuous maid, the daughter of a count
That died some twelvemonth since; then leaving her
In the protection of his son, her brother,
Who shortly also died: for whose dear love,
They say, she hath abjured the company
And sight of men.

VIO.   O that I served that lady,
And might not be delivered to the world,
Till I had made mine own occasion mellow,
What my estate is![2]

CAP.   That were hard to compass;
Because she will admit no kind of suit,
No, not the Duke's.

VIO.   There is a fair behaviour in thee, captain;

---

1. *Duke*] Orsino is subsequently spoken of merely as "Count."
2. *O...is!*] Viola wishes it were possible to keep her name and rank a secret until she chooses to make it known.

And though that nature with a beauteous wall
Doth oft close in pollution, yet of thee
I will believe thou hast a mind that suits
With this thy fair and outward character.
I prithee, and I 'll pay thee bounteously,
Conceal me what I am, and be my aid
For such disguise as haply shall become
The form of my intent. I 'll serve this Duke:
Thou shalt present me as an eunuch to him:
It may be worth thy pains; for I can sing,
And speak to him in many sorts of music,
That will allow me very worth his service.
What else may hap to time I will commit;
Only shape thou thy silence to my wit.

CAP. Be you his eunuch, and your mute I 'll be:
When my tongue blabs, then let mine eyes not see.

VIO. I thank thee: lead me on. [*Exeunt.*]

SCENE III. OLIVIA'S *house.*

Enter SIR TOBY BELCH *and* MARIA

SIR TO. What a plague means my niece, to take the death of her
brother thus? I am sure care 's an enemy to life.

MAR. By my troth, Sir Toby, you must come in earlier o' nights: your
cousin, my lady, takes great exceptions to your ill hours.

SIR TO. Why, let her except, before excepted.

MAR. Ay, but you must confine yourself within the modest limits of
order.

SIR TO. Confine! I 'll confine myself no finer than I am: these clothes
are good enough to drink in; and so be these boots too: an they be
not, let them hang themselves in their own straps.

MAR. That quaffing and drinking will undoe you: I heard my lady
talk of it yesterday; and of a foolish knight that you brought in one
night here to be her wooer.

SIR TO. Who, Sir Andrew Aguecheek?

MAR. Ay, he.

SIR TO.   He 's as tall a man as any 's in Illyria.

MAR.   What 's that to the purpose?

SIR TO.   Why, he has three thousand ducats a year.

MAR.   Ay, but he 'll have but a year in all these ducats: he 's a very fool and a prodigal.

SIR TO.   Fie, that you 'll say so! he plays o' the viol-de-gamboys, and speaks three or four languages word for word without book, and hath all the good gifts of nature.

MAR.   He hath indeed, almost natural: for besides that he 's a fool, he 's a great quarreller; and but that he hath the gift of a coward to allay the gust he hath in quarrelling, 't is thought among the prudent he would quickly have the gift of a grave.

SIR TO.   By this hand, they are scoundrels and substractors that say so of him. Who are they?

MAR.   They that add, moreover, he 's drunk nightly in your company.

SIR TO.   With drinking healths to my niece: I 'll drink to her as long as there is a passage in my throat and drink in Illyria: he 's a coward and a coystrill[1] that will not drink to my niece till his brains turn o' the toe like a parish-top.[2] What, wench! Castiliano vulgo;[3] for here comes Sir Andrew Agueface.

Enter SIR ANDREW AGUECHEEK

SIR AND.   Sir Toby Belch! how now, Sir Toby Belch!

SIR TO.   Sweet Sir Andrew!

SIR AND.   Bless you, fair shrew.

MAR.   And you too, sir.

SIR TO.   Accost, Sir Andrew, accost.

SIR AND.   What 's that?

SIR TO.   My niece's chambermaid.

SIR AND.   Good Mistress Accost, I desire better acquaintance.

MAR.   My name is Mary, sir.

SIR AND.   Good Mistress Mary Accost, —

SIR TO.   You mistake, knight: "accost" is front her, board her, woo her, assail her.

SIR AND.   By my troth, I would not undertake her in this company. Is that the meaning of "accost"?

---

1. *coystrill*] a common term of contempt, meaning "a base fellow."

2. *parish-top*] A large top provided by the parochial authorities in Shakespeare's day for boys to play with.

3. *Castiliano vulgo*] literally, the Spanish for "Castilian people."

MAR. Fare you well, gentlemen.

SIR TO. An thou let part so, Sir Andrew, would thou mightst never draw sword again.

SIR AND. An you part so, mistress, I would I might never draw sword again. Fair lady, do you think you have fools in hand?

MAR. Sir, I have not you by the hand.

SIR AND. Marry, but you shall have; and here 's my hand.

MAR. Now, sir, "thought is free": I pray you, bring your hand to the buttery-bar[4] and let it drink.

SIR AND. Wherefore, sweet-heart? what 's your metaphor?

MAR. It 's dry,[5] sir.

SIR AND. Why, I think so: I am not such an ass but I can keep my hand dry. But what 's your jest?

MAR. A dry jest,[6] sir.

SIR AND. Are you full of them?

MAR. Ay, sir, I have them at my fingers' ends: marry, now I let go your hand, I am barren.[7] [*Exit.*]

SIR TO. O knight, thou lackest a cup of canary:[8] when did I see thee so put down?

SIR AND. Never in your life, I think; unless you see canary put me down. Methinks sometimes I have no more wit than a Christian or an ordinary man has: but I am a great eater of beef and I believe that does harm to my wit.

SIR TO. No question.

SIR AND. An I thought that, I 'ld forswear it. I 'll ride home to-morrow, Sir Toby.

SIR TO. Pourquoi, my dear knight?

SIR AND. What is "pourquoi"? do or not do? I would I had bestowed that time in the tongues[9] that I have in fencing, dancing and bear-baiting: O, had I but followed the arts!

SIR TO. Then had'st thou had an excellent head of hair.

SIR AND. Why, would that have mended my hair?

---

4. *buttery-bar*] a room where provisions are stored.

5. *It 's dry*] A dry hand was commonly held to be a sign of indifference to love, as well as of debility and old age. A moist hand was commonly taken to be the sign of an amorous disposition.

6. *A dry jest*] An insipid jest.

7. *barren*] dull, witless, tedious.

8. *canary*] a sweet wine from the Canary Islands.

9. *in the tongues*] studying languages; "tongues" was often written and commonly pronounced as "tongs," and Sir Toby's retort about Sir Andrew's "head of hair" obviously shows that a pun on "tongs" in the sense of curling irons was intended.

SIR TO.   Past question; for thou seest it will not curl by nature.

SIR AND.   But it becomes me well enough, does 't not?

SIR TO.   Excellent; it hangs like flax on a distaff; and I hope to see a housewife take thee between her legs and spin it off.

SIR AND.   Faith, I 'll home to-morrow, Sir Toby: your niece will not be seen; or if she be, it 's four to one she 'll none of me: the count himself here hard by woos her.

SIR TO.   She 'll none o' the count: she 'll not match above her degree, neither in estate, years, nor wit; I have heard her swear 't. Tut, there 's life in 't, man.

SIR AND.   I 'll stay a month longer. I am a fellow o' the strangest mind i' the world; I delight in masques and revels sometimes altogether.

SIR TO.   Art thou good at these kickshawses,[10] knight?

SIR AND.   As any man in Illyria, whatsoever he be, under the degree of my betters; and yet I will not compare with an old man.

SIR TO.   What is thy excellence in a galliard, knight?

SIR AND.   Faith, I can cut a caper.[11]

SIR TO.   And I can cut the mutton to 't.

SIR AND.   And I think I have the back-trick simply as strong as any man in Illyria.

SIR TO.   Wherefore are these things hid? wherefore have these gifts a curtain before 'em? are they like to take dust, like Mistress Mall's picture? why dost thou not go to church in a galliard and come home in a coranto?[12] My very walk should be a jig; I would not so much as make water but in a sink-a-pace.[13] What dost thou mean? Is it a world to hide virtues in? I did think, by the excellent constitution of thy leg, it was formed under the star of a galliard.

SIR AND.   Ay, 't is strong, and it does indifferent well in a flame-coloured stock. Shall we set about some revels?

SIR TO.   What shall we do else? were we not born under Taurus?

SIR AND.   Taurus! That 's sides and heart.

SIR TO.   No, sir; it is legs and thighs.[14] Let me see thee caper: ha! higher: ha, ha! excellent!   [*Exeunt.*]

---

10. *kickshawses*] toys, trifles.

11. *galliard . . . caper*] lively dances.

12. *coranto*] another lively dance.

13. *sink-a-pace*] a phonetic spelling of "cinque pace," a lively dance.

14. *Taurus . . . thighs*] Astrology assumed that each part of the body was under the control of one or other signs of the zodiac. But both Sir Andrew and Sir Toby are in error in their reference to Taurus, who, according to the authorities, controls neither the "sides and hearts" nor the "legs and thighs," but the neck and throat.

Scene IV. *The* Duke's *palace.*

Enter Valentine, *and* Viola *in man's attire*

VAL. If the Duke continue these favours towards you, Cesario,[1] you are like to be much advanced: he hath known you but three days, and already you are no stranger.

VIO. You either fear his humour or my negligence, that you call in question the continuance of his love: is he constant, sir, in his favours?

VAL. No, believe me.

VIO. I thank you. Here comes the count.[2]

Enter Duke, Curio, *and* Attendants

DUKE. Who saw Cesario, ho?

VIO. On your attendance, my lord; here.

DUKE. Stand you a while aloof. Cesario,
Thou know'st no less but all; I have unclasp'd
To thee the book even of my secret soul:
Therefore, good youth, address thy gait unto her;
Be not denied access, stand at her doors,
And tell them, there thy fixed foot shall grow
Till thou have audience.

VIO.   Sure, my noble lord,
If she be so abandon'd to her sorrow
As it is spoke, she never will admit me.

DUKE. Be clamorous and leap all civil bounds
Rather than make unprofited return.

VIO. Say I do speak with her, my lord, what then?

DUKE. O, then unfold the passion of my love,
Surprise her with discourse of my dear faith:
It shall become thee well to act my woes;
She will attend it better in thy youth
Than in a nuncio's[3] of more grave aspect.

---

1. *Cesario*] Viola's male alias.
2. *the count*] In the stage directions throughout the play, Orsino is called "Duke," and is so spoken of at I, ii, 25. But everywhere else in the text he is referred to as "the count."
3. *nuncio's*] messenger's.

VIO. I think not so, my lord.
DUKE.   Dear lad, believe it;
  For they shall yet belie thy happy years,
  That say thou art a man: Diana's lip
  Is not more smooth and rubious;⁴ thy small pipe
  Is as the maiden's organ, shrill and sound;
  And all is semblative⁵ a woman's part.
  I know thy constellation is right apt
  For this affair. Some four or five attend him;
  All, if you will; for I myself am best
  When least in company. Prosper well in this,
  And thou shalt live as freely as thy lord,
  To call his fortunes thine.
VIO.   I 'll do my best
  To woo your lady: [*Aside*] yet, a barful⁶ strife!
  Whoe'er I woo, myself would be his wife.   [*Exeunt.*]

SCENE V. OLIVIA'S *house*.

Enter MARIA *and* Clown

MAR. Nay, either tell me where thou hast been, or I will not open my
      lips so wide as a bristle may enter in way of thy excuse: my lady
      will hang thee for thy absence.
CLO. Let her hang me: he that is well hanged in this world needs to
      fear no colours.¹
MAR. Make that good.
CLO. He shall see none to fear.
MAR. A good lenten² answer: I can tell thee where that saying was
      born, of "I fear no colours."
CLO. Where, good Mistress Mary?

---

4. *rubious*] apparently a once-used word; formed from "ruby."
5. *semblative*] like or similar to.
6. *barful*] full of obstacles.

---

1. *fear no colours*] fear no enemies; "colours" were ensigns or standards, which would have
   been displayed during battles.
2. *lenten*] scanty, spare.

MAR. In the wars; and that may you be bold to say in your foolery.

CLO. Well, God give them wisdom that have it; and those that are fools, let them use their talents.

MAR. Yet you will be hanged for being so long absent; or, to be turned away, is not that as good as a hanging to you?

CLO. Many a good hanging prevents a bad marriage; and, for turning away, let summer bear it out.³

MAR. You are resolute, then?

CLO. Not so, neither; but I am resolved on two points.

MAR. That if one break, the other will hold; or, if both break, your gaskins fall.⁴

CLO. Apt, in good faith; very apt. Well, go thy way; if Sir Toby would leave drinking, thou wert as witty a piece of Eve's flesh as any in Illyria.

MAR. Peace, you rogue, no more o' that. Here comes my lady: make your excuse wisely, you were best.   [*Exit.*]

CLO. Wit, an 't be thy will, put me into good fooling! Those wits, that think they have thee, do very oft prove fools; and I, that am sure I lack thee, may pass for a wise man: for what says Quinapalus?⁵ "Better a witty fool than a foolish wit."

Enter LADY OLIVIA *with* MALVOLIO

God bless thee, lady!

OLI. Take the fool away.

CLO. Do you not hear, fellows? Take away the lady.

OLI. Go to, you 're a dry fool; I 'll no more of you: besides, you grow dishonest.

CLO. Two faults, madonna, that drink and good counsel will amend: for give the dry fool drink, then is the fool not dry: bid the dishonest man mend himself; if he mend, he is no longer dishonest; if he cannot, let the botcher mend him. Any thing that 's mended is but patched: virtue that transgresses is but patched with sin; and sin that amends is but patched with virtue. If that this simple syllogism will serve, so; if it will not, what remedy? As there is no true cuckold but calamity, so beauty 's a flower. The lady bade take away the fool; therefore, I say again, take her away.

---

3. *for turning . . . out*] If I am threatened with dismissal, let us wait for next season,—next summer,—and see if the threat take effect, i.e., wait awhile and see.

4. *points . . . fall*] a "point" was a metal hook or tag, which attaches the gaskins, i.e., breeches or hose, to the doublet.

5. *Quinapalus*] An apocryphal philosopher invented for the occasion.

OLI. Sir, I bade them take away you.

CLO. Misprision[6] in the highest degree! Lady, cucullus non facit monachum;[7] that 's as much to say as I wear not motley in my brain. Good madonna, give me leave to prove you a fool.

OLI. Can you do it?

CLO. Dexteriously,[8] good madonna.

OLI. Make your proof.

CLO. I must catechize you for it, madonna: good my mouse of virtue, answer me.

OLI. Well, sir, for want of other idleness, I 'll bide your proof.

CLO. Good madonna, why mournest thou?

OLI. Good fool, for my brother's death.

CLO. I think his soul is in hell, madonna.

OLI. I know his soul is in heaven, fool.

CLO. The more fool, madonna, to mourn for your brother's soul being in heaven. Take away the fool, gentlemen.

OLI. What think you of this fool, Malvolio? doth he not mend?

MAL. Yes, and shall do till the pangs of death shake him: infirmity, that decays the wise, doth ever make the better fool.

CLO. God send you, sir, a speedy infirmity, for the better increasing your folly! Sir Toby will be sworn that I am no fox; but he will not pass his word for two pence that you are no fool.

OLI. How say you to that, Malvolio?

MAL. I marvel your ladyship takes delight in such a barren rascal: I saw him put down the other day with an ordinary fool that has no more brain than a stone. Look you now, he 's out of his guard already; unless you laugh and minister occasion to him, he is gagged. I protest, I take these wise men, that crow so at these set kind of fools, no better than the fools' zanies.[9]

OLI. O, you are sick of self-love, Malvolio, and taste with a distempered appetite. To be generous, guiltless and of free disposition, is to take those things for bird-bolts[10] that you deem cannon-bullets: there is no slander in an allowed fool, though he do nothing but

---

6. *Misprision*] Legally the term "misprision," which literally means "contempt," was applied to evil speaking of the sovereign.

7. *cucullus . . . monachum*] "The cowl does not make the monk," a proverb in vogue throughout Europe.

8. *Dexteriously*] Dexterously.

9. *zanies*] a subordinate buffoon whose duty was to make awkward attempts at mimicking the tricks of the professional clown.

10. *bird-bolts*] short arrows with broad flat ends, used to kill birds without piercing them.

rail; nor no railing in a known discreet man, though he do nothing but reprove.

CLO. Now Mercury endue thee with leasing,[11] for thou speakest well of fools!

Re-enter MARIA

MAR. Madam, there is at the gate a young gentleman much desires to speak with you.

OLI. From the Count Orsino, is it?

MAR. I know not, madam: 't is a fair young man, and well attended.

OLI. Who of my people hold him in delay?

MAR. Sir Toby, madam, your kinsman.

OLI. Fetch him off, I pray you; he speaks nothing but madman: fie on him! [*Exit* MARIA.] Go you, Malvolio: if it be a suit from the count, I am sick, or not at home; what you will, to dismiss it. [*Exit* MALVOLIO.] Now you see, sir, how your fooling grows old, and people dislike it.

CLO. Thou hast spoke for us, madonna, as if thy eldest son should be a fool; whose skull Jove cram with brains! for, —here he comes, — one of thy kin has a most weak pia mater.[12]

Enter SIR TOBY

OLI. By mine honour, half drunk. What is he at the gate, cousin?

SIR TO. A gentleman.

OLI. A gentleman! what gentleman?

SIR TO. 'T is a gentleman here—a plague o' these pickle-herring![13] How now, sot!

CLO. Good Sir Toby!

OLI. Cousin, cousin, how have you come so early by this lethargy?

SIR TO. Lechery! I defy lechery. There 's one at the gate.

OLI. Ay, marry, what is he?

SIR TO. Let him be the devil, an he will, I care not: give me faith, say I. Well, it 's all one. [*Exit.*]

OLI. What 's a drunken man like, fool?

CLO. Like a drowned man, a fool and a mad man: one draught above

---

11. *Mercury . . . leasing*] May the god of cheats or liars endow thee, to thy profit, with the gift of lying.
12. *pia mater*] the membrane that covers the brain; the term was used for the brain itself.
13. *pickle-herring*] the favourite relish for drunkards.

heat[14] makes him a fool; the second mads him; and a third drowns him.

OLI.   Go thou and seek the crowner,[15] and let him sit o' my coz; for he 's in the third degree of drink, he 's drowned: go look after him.

CLO.   He is but mad yet, madonna; and the fool shall look to the mad-man.   [*Exit.*]

Re-enter MALVOLIO

MAL.   Madam, yond young fellow swears he will speak with you. I told him you were sick; he takes on him to understand so much, and therefore comes to speak with you. I told him you were asleep; he seems to have a foreknowledge of that too, and therefore comes to speak with you. What is to be said to him, lady? he 's fortified against any denial.

OLI.   Tell him he shall not speak with me.

MAL.   Has been told so; and he says, he 'll stand at your door like a sheriff's post,[16] and be the supporter to a bench, but he 'll speak with you.

OLI.   What kind o' man is he?

MAL.   Why, of mankind.

OLI.   What manner of man?

MAL.   Of very ill manner; he 'll speak with you, will you or no.

OLI.   Of what personage and years is he?

MAL.   Not yet old enough for a man, nor young enough for a boy; as a squash is before 't is a peascod, or a codling[17] when 't is almost an apple: 't is with him in standing water,[18] between boy and man. He is very well-favoured and he speaks very shrewishly; one would think his mother's milk were scarce out of him.

OLI.   Let him approach: call in my gentlewoman.

MAL.   Gentlewoman, my lady calls.   [*Exit.*]

Re-enter MARIA

OLI.   Give me my veil: come, throw it o'er my face. We 'll once more hear Orsino's embassy.

---

14. *above heat*] above ordinary strength.

15. *crowner*] coroner.

16. *sheriff's post*] a post, often carved with elaborate ornament, which stood before the door of the house occupied by a city mayor and sheriff.

17. *squash . . . codling*] terms respectively for an unripe peascod and an unripe apple.

18. *in standing water*] just at the turn of the tide, in the condition of stationary water that neither ebbs nor flows.

Enter VIOLA, *and* Attendants

VIO. The honourable lady of the house, which is she?

OLI. Speak to me; I shall answer for her. Your will?

VIO. Most radiant, exquisite and unmatchable beauty,—I pray you, tell me if this be the lady of the house, for I never saw her: I would be loath to cast away my speech, for besides that it is excellently well penned, I have taken great pains to con it. Good beauties, let me sustain no scorn; I am very comptible,[19] even to the least sinister usage.

OLI. Whence came you, sir?

VIO. I can say little more than I have studied, and that question's out of my part. Good gentle one, give me modest assurance if you be the lady of the house, that I may proceed in my speech.

OLI. Are you a comedian?

VIO. No, my profound heart: and yet, by the very fangs of malice I swear, I am not that I play. Are you the lady of the house?

OLI. If I do not usurp myself, I am.

VIO. Most certain, if you are she, you do usurp yourself; for what is yours to bestow is not yours to reserve. But this is from my commission: I will on with my speech in your praise, and then show you the heart of my message.

OLI. Come to what is important in 't: I forgive you the praise.

VIO. Alas, I took great pains to study it, and 't is poetical.

OLI. It is the more like to be feigned: I pray you, keep it in. I heard you were saucy at my gates, and allowed your approach rather to wonder at you than to hear you. If you be not mad, be gone; if you have reason, be brief: 't is not that time of moon with me to make one in so skipping a dialogue.[20]

MAR. Will you hoist sail, sir? here lies your way.

VIO. No, good swabber;[21] I am to hull[22] here a little longer. Some mollification for your giant,[23] sweet lady. Tell me your mind: I am a messenger.

---

19. *comptible*] sensitive.

20. *'t is . . . dialogue*] the waning and waxing of the moon served as images of change; the sense here is that Olivia is in no mood or humor to entertain any flighty or thoughtless (skipping) exchange with Viola/Cassio.

21. *swabber*] one who mops the ship's deck at sea.

22. *hull*] drift with the sails furled.

23. *giant*] an ironical reference to Maria, who, as implied elsewhere in the play, is small in size.

OLI.   Sure, you have some hideous matter to deliver, when the courtesy of it is so fearful. Speak your office.

VIO.   It alone concerns your ear. I bring no overture of war, no taxa-
tion of homage: I hold the olive in my hand; my words are as full
of peace as matter.

OLI.   Yet you began rudely. What are you? what would you?

VIO.   The rudeness that hath appeared in me have I learned from my
entertainment. What I am, and what I would, are as secret as
maidenhead; to your ears, divinity, to any other's, profanation.

OLI.   Give us the place alone: we will hear this divinity. [*Exeunt*
MARIA *and* Attendants.] Now, sir, what is your text?

VIO.   Most sweet lady,—

OLI.   A comfortable doctrine, and much may be said of it. Where lies
your text?

VIO.   In Orsino's bosom.

OLI.   In his bosom! In what chapter of his bosom?

VIO.   To answer by the method, in the first of his heart.

OLI.   O, I have read it: it is heresy. Have you no more to say?

VIO.   Good madam, let me see your face.

OLI.   Have you any commission from your lord to negotiate with my
face? You are now out of your text: but we will draw the curtain
and show you the picture. Look you, sir, such a one I was this present: is 't not well done?   [*Unveiling.*]

VIO.   Excellently done, if God did all.

OLI.   'T is in grain,[24] sir; 't will endure wind and weather.

VIO.   'T is beauty truly blent, whose red and white
Nature's own sweet and cunning hand laid on:
Lady, you are the cruell'st she alive,
If you will lead these graces to the grave
And leave the world no copy.

OLI.   O, sir, I will not be so hard-hearted; I will give out divers sched-
ules of my beauty: it shall be inventoried, and every particle and
utensil labelled to my will: as, item, two lips, indifferent red; item,
two grey eyes, with lids to them; item, one neck, one chin, and so
forth. Were you sent hither to praise me?

VIO.   I see you what you are, you are too proud;
But, if you were the devil, you are fair.
My lord and master loves you: O, such love
Could be but recompensed, though you were crown'd

---

24. *in grain*] of a fast dye that will not wash out.

The nonpareil of beauty!

OLI.   How does he love me?

VIO.   With adorations, fertile tears,
   With groans that thunder love, with sighs of fire.

OLI.   Your lord does know my mind; I cannot love him:
   Yet I suppose him virtuous, know him noble,
   Of great estate, of fresh and stainless youth;
   In voices well divulged,[25] free, learn'd and valiant;
   And in dimension and the shape of nature
   A gracious person; but yet I cannot love him;
   He might have took his answer long ago.

VIO.   If I did love you in my master's flame,
   With such a suffering, such a deadly life,
   In your denial I would find no sense;
   I would not understand it.

OLI.   Why, what would you?

VIO.   Make me a willow cabin at your gate,
   And call upon my soul within the house;
   Write loyal cantons of contemned love
   And sing them loud even in the dead of night;
   Halloo your name to the reverberate hills,
   And make the babbling gossip of the air
   Cry out "Olivia!" O, you should not rest
   Between the elements of air and earth,
   But you should pity me!

OLI.   You might do much.
   What is your parentage?

VIO.   Above my fortunes, yet my state is well:
   I am a gentleman.

OLI.   Get you to your lord;
   I cannot love him: let him send no more;
   Unless, perchance, you come to me again,
   To tell me how he takes it. Fare you well:
   I thank you for your pains: spend this for me.

VIO.   I am no fee'd post,[26] lady; keep your purse:
   My master, not myself, lacks recompense.
   Love make his heart of flint that you shall love;
   And let your fervour, like my master's, be

---

25. *well divulged*] well spoken of by the world.
26. *fee'd post*] hired messenger.

      Placed in contempt! Farewell, fair cruelty.   [*Exit.*]
OLI.   "What is your parentage?"
      "Above my fortunes, yet my state is well:
      I am a gentleman." I 'll be sworn thou art;
      Thy tongue, thy face, thy limbs, actions, and spirit,
      Do give thee five-fold blazon:[27] not too fast: soft, soft!
      Unless the master were the man. How now!
      Even so quickly may one catch the plague?
      Methinks I feel this youth's perfections
      With an invisible and subtle stealth
      To creep in at mine eyes. Well, let it be.
      What ho, Malvolio!

Re-enter MALVOLIO

MAL.   Here, madam, at your service.
OLI.   Run after that same peevish messenger,
      The county's man: he left this ring behind him,
      Would I or not: tell him I 'll none of it.
      Desire him not to flatter with his lord,
      Nor hold him up with hopes; I am not for him:
      If that the youth will come this way to-morrow,
      I 'll give him reasons for 't: hie thee, Malvolio.
MAL.   Madam, I will.   [*Exit.*]
OLI.   I do I know not what, and fear to find
      Mine eye too great a flatterer for my mind.
      Fate, show thy force: ourselves we do not owe;
      What is decreed must be, and be this so.   [*Exit.*]

---

27. *blazon*] coat of arms.

ACT II

Scene I. *The sea-coast.*

Enter ANTONIO *and* SEBASTIAN

ANT.　Will you stay no longer? nor will you not that I go with you?

SEB.　By your patience, no. My stars shine darkly over me: the malignancy of my fate might perhaps distemper yours; therefore I shall crave of you your leave that I may bear my evils alone: it were a bad recompense for your love, to lay any of them on you.

ANT.　Let me yet know of you whither you are bound.

SEB.　No, sooth, sir: my determinate voyage is mere extravagancy.[1] But I perceive in you so excellent a touch of modesty, that you will not extort from me what I am willing to keep in; therefore it charges me in manners the rather to express myself. You must know of me then, Antonio, my name is Sebastian, which I called Roderigo. My father was that Sebastian of Messaline, whom I know you have heard of. He left behind him myself and a sister, both born in an hour: if the heavens had been pleased, would we had so ended! but you, sir, altered that; for some hour before you took me from the breach of the sea was my sister drowned.

ANT.　Alas the day!

SEB.　A lady, sir, though it was said she much resembled me, was yet of many accounted beautiful: but, though I could not with such estimable wonder overfar believe that, yet thus far I will boldly publish her; she bore a mind that envy could not but call fair. She is drowned already, sir, with salt water, though I seem to drown her remembrance again with more.

ANT.　Pardon me, sir, your bad entertainment.

SEB.　O good Antonio, forgive me your trouble.

ANT.　If you will not murder me for my love, let me be your servant.

SEB.　If you will not undo what you have done, that is, kill him whom you have recovered, desire it not. Fare ye well at once: my bosom is full of kindness, and I am yet so near the manners of my moth-

---

1. *my determinate . . . extravagancy*] The voyage I have resolved upon is mere vagrancy, mere roaming.

er, that upon the least occasion more mine eyes will tell tales of
me. I am bound to the Count Orsino's court: farewell.   [*Exit.*]
ANT.   The gentleness of all the gods go with thee!
I have many enemies in Orsino's court,
Else would I very shortly see thee there.
But, come what may, I do adore thee so,
That danger shall seem sport, and I will go.   [*Exit.*]

SCENE II. *A street.*

Enter VIOLA, MALVOLIO *following*

MAL.   Were not you even now with the Countess Olivia?
VIO.   Even now, sir; on a moderate pace I have since arrived but hither.
MAL.   She returns this ring to you, sir: you might have saved me my
pains, to have taken it away yourself. She adds, moreover, that you
should put your lord into a desperate assurance she will none of
him: and one thing more, that you be never so hardy to come
again in his affairs, unless it be to report your lord's taking of this.
Receive it so.
VIO.   She took the ring of me: I 'll none of it.
MAL.   Come, sir, you peevishly threw it to her; and her will is, it
should be so returned: if it be worth stooping for, there it lies in
your eye; if not, be it his that finds it.   [*Exit.*]
VIO.   I left no ring with her: what means this lady?
Fortune forbid my outside have not charm'd her!
She made good view of me; indeed, so much,
That methought her eyes had lost her tongue,
For she did speak in starts distractedly.
She loves me, sure; the cunning of her passion
Invites me in this churlish messenger.
None of my lord's ring! why, he sent her none.
I am the man: if it be so, as 't is,
Poor lady, she were better love a dream.
Disguise, I see, thou art a wickedness,

Wherein the pregnant enemy[1] does much.
How easy is it for the proper-false
In women's waxen hearts to set their forms!
Alas, our frailty is the cause, not we!
For such as we are made of, such we be.
How will this fadge?[2] my master loves her dearly;
And I, poor monster, fond as much on him;
And she, mistaken, seems to dote on me.
What will become of this? As I am man,
My state is desperate for my master's love;
As I am woman,—now alas the day!—
What thriftless sighs shall poor Olivia breathe!
O time! thou must untangle this, not I;
It is too hard a knot for me to untie!　　　　　　　　　　[*Exit.*]

SCENE III. OLIVIA's *house.*

Enter SIR TOBY *and* SIR ANDREW

SIR TO.　　Approach, Sir Andrew: not to be a-bed after midnight is to be up betimes; and "diluculo surgere,"[1] thou know'st,—

SIR AND.　　Nay, by my troth, I know not: but I know, to be up late is to be up late.

SIR TO.　　A false conclusion: I hate it as an unfilled can. To be up after midnight and to go to bed then, is early: so that to go to bed after midnight is to go to bed betimes. Does not our life consist of the four elements?

SIR AND.　　Faith, so they say; but I think it rather consists of eating and drinking.

SIR TO.　　Thou 'rt a scholar; let us therefore eat and drink. Marian, I say! a stoup of wine!

Enter Clown

---

1. *the pregnant enemy*] the alert enemy of mankind, i.e., the devil.
2. *fadge*] turn out.

1. *"diluculo surgere"*] *sc.* saluberrimum est, "To rise at dawn is very healthy."

Sir And.   Here comes the fool, i' faith.

Clo.   How now, my hearts! did you never see the picture of "we three"?[2]

Sir To.   Welcome, ass. Now let 's have a catch.[3]

Sir And.   By my troth, the fool has an excellent breast. I had rather than forty shillings I had such a leg, and so sweet a breath to sing, as the fool has. In sooth, thou wast in very gracious fooling last night, when thou spokest of Pigrogromitus, of the Vapians passing the equinoctial of Queubus:[4] 't was very good, i' faith. I sent thee sixpence for thy leman:[5] hadst it?

Clo.   I did impeticos thy gratillity; for Malvolio's nose is no whipstock: my lady has a white hand, and the Myrmidons are no bottle-ale houses.[6]

Sir And.   Excellent! why, this is the best fooling, when all is done. Now, a song.

Sir To.   Come on; there is sixpence for you: let 's have a song.

Sir And.   There 's a testril[7] of me too: if one knight give a —

Clo.   Would you have a love-song, or a song of good life?

Sir To.   A love-song, a love-song.

Sir And.   Ay, ay: I care not for good life.

Clo.   [Sings]

> O mistress mine, where are you roaming?
> O, stay and hear; your true love's coming,
>   That can sing both high and low:
> Trip no further, pretty sweeting;
> Journeys end in lovers meeting,
>   Every wise man's son doth know.

Sir And.   Excellent good, i' faith.

Sir To.   Good, good.

---

2. *picture of "we three"*] a common ale-house sign on which was painted the heads of two fools, or two asses, with the legend "We three logger-heads be." The spectator makes up the trio.

3. *a catch*] a song sung in succession, i.e. a round.

4. *Pigrogromitus . . . Queubus*] proper names invented for the occasion.

5. *leman*] lover.

6. *I did impeticos . . . houses*] The clown talks nonsense to something of this effect: "I impocketed thy diminutive gratuity (or I gave it to my petticoat companion). Malvolio's inquisitive nose may smell out our sins, but cannot punish them. My sweetheart is a lady of refinement, and the myrmidons, the humbler retainers of a noble household, are not of the vulgar and coarse character attaching to pot-houses."

7. *testril*] sixpence.

CLO. [*Sings*]

> What is love? 't is not hereafter;
> Present mirth hath present laughter;
>   What 's to come is still unsure:
> In delay there lies no plenty;
> Then come kiss me, sweet and twenty,
>   Youth 's a stuff will not endure.

SIR AND. A mellifluous voice, as I am true knight.

SIR TO. A contagious breath.

SIR AND. Very sweet and contagious, i' faith.

SIR TO. To hear by the nose, it is dulcet in contagion. But shall we make the welkin dance indeed? shall we rouse the night-owl in a catch that will draw three souls out of one weaver?[8] shall we do that?

SIR AND. An you love me, let 's do 't: I am dog at a catch.

CLO. By 'r lady, sir, and some dogs will catch well.

SIR AND. Most certain. Let our catch be, "Thou knave."

CLO. "Hold thy peace, thou knave," knight? I shall be constrained in 't to call thee knave, knight.

SIR AND. 'T is not the first time I have constrained one to call me knave. Begin, fool: it begins "Hold thy peace."

CLO. I shall never begin if I hold my peace.

SIR AND. Good, i' faith. Come, begin.   [*Catch sung.*]

Enter MARIA

MAR. What a caterwauling do you keep here! If my lady have not called up her steward Malvolio and bid him turn you out of doors, never trust me.

SIR TO. My lady 's a Cataian,[9] we are politicians, Malvolio 's a Peg-a-Ramsey, and "Three merry men be we."[10] Am not I consanguineous? am I not of her blood? Tillyvally. Lady! [*Sings*] "There dwelt a man in Babylon, lady, lady!"

CLO. Beshrew me, the knight 's in admirable fooling.

SIR AND. Ay, he does well enough if he be disposed, and so do I too: he does it with a better grace, but I do it more natural.

SIR TO. [*Sings*] "O, the twelfth day of December,"—

---

8. *catch . . . weaver*] Weavers were commonly held to be good singers. The "catch that will draw three souls out of one weaver" must have rare powers of enchantment.

9. *a Cataian*] a Chinese person (used as a term of reproach).

10. *Peg-a-Ramsey. . . be we*"] songs.

MAR.   For the love o' God, peace!

Enter MALVOLIO

MAL.   My masters, are you mad? or what are you? Have you no wit, manners, nor honesty, but to gabble like tinkers at this time of night? Do ye make an ale-house of my lady's house, that ye squeak out your coziers'[11] catches without any mitigation or remorse of voice? Is there no respect of place, persons, nor time in you?

SIR TO.   We did keep time, sir, in our catches. Sneck up!

MAL.   Sir Toby, I must be round with you. My lady bade me tell you, that, though she harbours you as her kinsman, she 's nothing allied to your disorders. If you can separate yourself and your misdemeanours, you are welcome to the house; if not, an it would please you to take leave of her, she is very willing to bid you farewell.

SIR TO.   "Farewell, dear heart, since I must needs be gone."

MAR.   Nay, good Sir Toby.

CLO.   "His eyes do show his days are almost done."

MAL.   Is 't even so?

SIR TO.   "But I will never die."

CLO.   Sir Toby, there you lie.

MAL.   This is much credit to you.

SIR TO.   "Shall I bid him go?"

CLO.   "What an if you do?"

SIR TO.   "Shall I bid him go, and spare not?"

CLO.   "O no, no, no, no, you dare not."

SIR TO.   Out o' tune, sir: ye lie. Art any more than a steward? Dost thou think, because thou art virtuous, there shall be no more cakes and ale?

CLO.   Yes, by Saint Anne, and ginger shall be hot i' the mouth too.

SIR TO.   Thou 'rt i' the right. Go, sir, rub your chain[12] with crums. A stoup of wine, Maria!

MAL.   Mistress Mary, if you prized my lady's favour at any thing more than contempt, you would not give means for this uncivil rule: she shall know of it, by this hand.   [*Exit.*]

MAR.   Go shake your ears.

SIR AND.   'T were as good a deed as to drink when a man 's a-hungry,

---

11. *coziers*'] cobblers'.
12. *rub your chain*] Stewards wore gold chains round their necks in right of their office.

to challenge him the field, and then to break promise with him and make a fool of him.

SIR TO. Do 't, knight: I 'll write thee a challenge; or I 'll deliver thy indignation to him by word of mouth.

MAR. Sweet Sir Toby, be patient for to-night: since the youth of the count's was to-day with my lady, she is much out of quiet. For Monsieur Malvolio, let me alone with him: if I do not gull him into a nayword,[13] and make him a common recreation, do not think I have wit enough to lie straight in my bed: I know I can do it.

SIR TO. Possess us, possess us; tell us something of him.

MAR. Marry, sir, sometimes he is a kind of puritan.

SIR AND. O, if I thought that, I 'ld beat him like a dog!

SIR TO. What, for being a puritan? thy exquisite reason, dear knight?

SIR AND. I have no exquisite reason for 't, but I have reason good enough.

MAR. The devil a puritan that he is, or any thing constantly, but a time-pleaser; an affectioned ass, that cons state without book and utters it by great swarths:[14] the best persuaded of himself, so crammed, as he thinks, with excellencies, that it is his grounds of faith that all that look on him love him; and on that vice in him will my revenge find notable cause to work.

SIR TO. What wilt thou do?

MAR. I will drop in his way some obscure epistles of love; wherein, by the colour of his beard, the shape of his leg, the manner of his gait, the expressure[15] of his eye, forehead, and complexion, he shall find himself most feelingly personated. I can write very like my lady your niece: on a forgotten matter we can hardly make distinction of our hands.

SIR TO. Excellent! I smell a device.

SIR AND. I have 't in my nose too.

SIR TO. He shall think, by the letters that thou wilt drop, that they come from my niece, and that she 's in love with him.

MAR. My purpose is, indeed, a horse of that colour.

SIR AND. And your horse now would make him an ass.

MAR. Ass, I doubt not.

SIR AND. O, 't will be admirable!

---

13. *gull him . . . nayword*] trick him so that he becomes a byword or laughing-stock.

14. *cons . . . swarths*] learns by heart gossip of state affairs and spouts it in great lengths or masses.

15. *expressure*] accurate description.

MAR. Sport royal, I warrant you: I know my physic will work with
      him. I will plant you two, and let the fool make a third, where he
      shall find the letter: observe his construction of it. For this night,
      to bed, and dream on the event. Farewell.   [*Exit.*]
SIR TO. Good night, Penthesilea.[16]
SIR AND. Before me, she 's a good wench.
SIR TO. She 's a beagle, true-bred, and one that adores me: what o'
      that?
SIR AND. I was adored once too.
SIR TO. Let 's to bed, knight. Thou hadst need send for more money.
SIR AND. If I cannot recover your niece, I am a foul way out.
SIR TO. Send for money, knight: if thou hast her not i' the end, call
      me cut.[17]
SIR AND. If I do not, never trust me, take it how you will.
SIR TO. Come, come, I 'll go burn some sack; 't is too late to go to
      bed now: come, knight; come, knight.   [*Exeunt.*]

SCENE IV. *The* DUKE'S *palace.*

Enter DUKE, VIOLA, CURIO, *and others*

DUKE. Give me some music. Now, good morrow, friends.
      Now, good Cesario, but that piece of song,
      That old and antique song we heard last night:
      Methought it did relieve my passion much,
      More than light airs and recollected terms[1]
      Of these most brisk and giddy-paced times:
      Come, but one verse.
CUR. He is not here, so please your lordship, that should sing it.
DUKE. Who was it?
CUR. Feste, the jester, my lord; a fool that the lady Olivia's father took
      much delight in. He is about the house.
DUKE. Seek him out, and play the tune the while.

---

16. *Penthesilea*] Queen of the Amazons (another ironic reference to Maria's small size).
17. *cut*] a common expression of contempt, "cut" meaning a bobtailed horse.

---

1. *recollected terms*] studied or stilted expressions; phrases lacking spontaneity.

[*Exit* CURIO. *Music plays.*]

Come hither, boy: if ever thou shalt love,
In the sweet pangs of it remember me;
For such as I am all true lovers are,
Unstaid and skittish in all motions else,
Save in the constant image of the creature
That is beloved. How dost thou like this tune?

VIO.   It gives a very echo to the seat
Where Love is throned.

DUKE.   Thou dost speak masterly:
My life upon 't, young though thou art, thine eye
Hath stay'd upon some favour that it loves:
Hath it not, boy?

VIO.   A little, by your favour.

DUKE.   What kind of woman is 't?

VIO.   Of your complexion.

DUKE.   She is not worth thee, then. What years, i' faith?

VIO.   About your years, my lord.

DUKE.   Too old, by heaven: let still the woman take
An elder than herself; so wears she to him,
So sways she level in her husband's heart:
For, boy, however we do praise ourselves,
Our fancies are more giddy and unfirm,
More longing, wavering, sooner lost and worn,
Than women's are.

VIO.   I think it well, my lord.

DUKE.   Then let thy love be younger than thyself,
Or thy affection cannot hold the bent;
For women are as roses, whose fair flower
Being once display'd, doth fall that very hour.

VIO.   And so they are: alas, that they are so;
To die, even when they to perfection grow!

Re-enter CURIO *and* Clown

DUKE.   O, fellow, come, the song we had last night.
Mark it, Cesario, it is old and plain;
The spinsters and the knitters in the sun
And the free maids that weave their thread with bones
Do use to chant it: it is silly sooth,
And dallies with the innocence of love,

Like the old age.[2]

CLO. Are you ready, sir?

DUKE. Ay; prithee, sing.   [*Music.*]

SONG

CLO.   Come away, come away, death,
              And in sad cypress[3] let me be laid;
          Fly away, fly away, breath;
              I am slain by a fair cruel maid.
          My shroud of white, stuck all with yew,
                  O, prepare it!
          My part of death, no one so true
                  Did share it.

          Not a flower, not a flower sweet,
              On my black coffin let there be strown;
          Not a friend, not a friend greet
              My poor corpse, where my bones shall be thrown:
          A thousand thousand sighs to save,
                  Lay me, O, where
          Sad true lover never find my grave,
                  To weep there!

DUKE. There 's for thy pains.

CLO. No pains, sir; I take pleasure in singing, sir.

DUKE. I 'll pay thy pleasure then.

CLO. Truly, sir, and pleasure will be paid, one time or another.

DUKE. Give me now leave to leave thee.

CLO. Now, the melancholy god protect thee; and the tailor make thy
      doublet of changeable taffeta, for thy mind is a very opal. I would
      have men of such constancy put to sea, that their business might
      be every thing and their intent every where; for that 's it that always
      makes a good voyage of nothing. Farewell.   [*Exit.*]

DUKE. Let all the rest give place.   [CURIO *and* Attendants *retire.*]
                            Once more, Cesario,
      Get thee to yond same sovereign cruelty:
      Tell her, my love, more noble than the world,
      Prizes not quantity of dirty lands;
      The parts that fortune hath bestow'd upon her,
      Tell her, I hold as giddily as fortune;

------

2. *the old age*] times past.
3. *cypress*] coffin of cypress wood.

But 't is that miracle and queen of gems
That nature pranks her in attracts my soul.
VIO.   But if she cannot love you, sir?
DUKE.   I cannot be so answer'd.
VIO.   Sooth, but you must.
Say that some lady, as perhaps there is,
Hath for your love as great a pang of heart
As you have for Olivia: you cannot love her;
You tell her so; must she not then be answer'd?
DUKE.   There is no woman's sides
Can bide the beating of so strong a passion
As love doth give my heart; no woman's heart
So big, to hold so much; they lack retention.[4]
Alas, their love may be call'd appetite,—
No motion of the liver, but the palate,—
That suffer surfeit, cloyment[5] and revolt;
But mine is all as hungry as the sea,
And can digest as much: make no compare
Between that love a woman can bear me
And that I owe Olivia.
VIO.   Ay, but I know,—
DUKE.   What dost thou know?
VIO.   Too well what love women to men may owe:
In faith, they are as true of heart as we.
My father had a daughter loved a man,
As it might be, perhaps, were I a woman,
I should your lordship.
DUKE.   And what 's her history?
VIO.   A blank, my lord. She never told her love,
But let concealment, like a worm i' the bud,
Feed on her damask cheek: she pined in thought;
And with a green and yellow melancholy
She sat like patience on a monument,
Smiling at grief. Was not this love indeed?
We men may say more, swear more: but indeed
Our shows are more than will; for still we prove
Much in our vows, but little in our love.
DUKE.   But died thy sister of her love, my boy?

_____

4. *retention*] power of retaining.
5. *cloyment*] satiety.

Vio. I am all the daughters of my father's house,
      And all the brothers too: and yet I know not.
      Sir, shall I to this lady?
Duke.   Ay, that 's the theme.
      To her in haste; give her this jewel; say,
      My love can give no place, bide no denay.   [*Exeunt.*]

Scene V. Olivia's *garden.*

Enter Sir Toby, Sir Andrew, *and* Fabian

Sir To. Come thy ways, Signior Fabian.
Fab. Nay, I 'll come: if I lose a scruple of this sport, let me be boiled
      to death with melancholy.
Sir To. Wouldst thou not be glad to have the niggardly rascally
      sheep-biter[1] come by some notable shame?
Fab. I would exult, man: you know, he brought me out o' favour with
      my lady about a bear-baiting here.
Sir To. To anger him we 'll have the bear again; and we will fool him
      black and blue: shall we not, Sir Andrew?
Sir And. An we do not, it is pity of our lives.
Sir To. Here comes the little villain.

Enter Maria

      How now, my metal of India![2]
Mar. Get ye all three into the box-tree: Malvolio's coming down this
      walk: he has been yonder i' the sun practising behaviour to his
      own shadow this half hour: observe him, for the love of mockery;
      for I know this letter will make a contemplative idiot of him.
      Close, in the name of jesting! Lie thou there [*throws down a let-
      ter*]; for here comes the trout that must be caught with tickling.
                                                                [*Exit.*]

Enter Malvolio

---

1. *sheep-biter*] A contemptuous term derived from a dog that worries sheep by biting.
2. *my metal of India*] my treasure of gold.

MAL. 'T is but fortune; all is fortune. Maria once told me she[3] did affect me: and I have heard herself come thus near, that, should she fancy, it should be one of my complexion. Besides, she uses me with a more exalted respect than any one else that follows her. What should I think on 't?

SIR TO. Here's an overweening rogue!

FAB. O, peace! Contemplation makes a rare turkey-cock of him: how he jets under his advanced plumes!

SIR AND. 'Slight, I could so beat the rogue!

SIR TO. Peace, I say.

MAL. To be Count Malvolio!

SIR TO. Ah, rogue!

SIR AND. Pistol him, pistol him.

SIR TO. Peace, peace!

MAL. There is example for 't; the lady of the Strachy married the yeoman of the wardrobe.

SIR AND. Fie on him Jezebel!

FAB. O, peace! now he 's deeply in: look how imagination blows him.

MAL. Having been three months married to her, sitting in my state, —

SIR TO. O, for a stone-bow,[4] to hit him in the eye!

MAL. Calling my officers about me, in my branched velvet[5] gown; having come from a day-bed, where I have left Olivia sleeping, —

SIR TO. Fire and brimstone!

FAB. O, peace, peace!

MAL. And then to have the humour of state; and after a demure travel of regard, telling them I know my place as I would they should do theirs, to ask for my kinsman Toby, —

SIR TO. Bolts and shackles!

FAB. O, peace, peace, peace! now, now.

MAL. Seven of my people, with an obedient start, make out for him: I frown the while; and perchance wind up my watch, or play with my—some rich jewel. Toby approaches; courtesies there to me, —

SIR TO. Shall this fellow live?

FAB. Though our silence be drawn from us with cars,[6] yet peace.

MAL. I extend my hand to him thus, quenching my familiar smile with an austere regard of control, —

---

3. *she*] i. e., Olivia, Maria's mistress.
4. *stone-bow*] a cross-bow from which stones were shot.
5. *branched velvet*] velvet ornamented with patterns of leaves and flowers.
6. *cars*] as in teams of horses.

SIR TO.   And does not Toby take you a blow o' the lips then?

MAL.   Saying, "Cousin Toby, my fortunes having cast me on your niece give me this prerogative of speech,"—

SIR TO.   What, what?

MAL.   "You must amend your drunkenness."

SIR TO.   Out, scab!

FAB.   Nay, patience, or we break the sinews of our plot.

MAL.   "Besides, you waste the treasure of your time with a foolish knight,"—

SIR AND.   That's me, I warrant you.

MAL.   "One Sir Andrew,"—

SIR AND.   I knew 't was I; for many do call me fool.

MAL.   What employment[7] have we here?   [*Taking up the letter.*]

FAB.   Now is the woodcock near the gin.[8]

SIR TO.   O, peace! and the spirit of humours intimate reading aloud to him!

MAL.   By my life, this is my lady's hand: these be her very C's, her U's, and her T's; and thus makes she her great P's. It is, in contempt of question, her hand.

SIR AND.   Her C's, her U's and her T's: why that?

MAL.   [*Reads*] To the unknown beloved, this, and my good wishes:—her very phrases! By your leave, wax. Soft! and the impressure her Lucrece,[9] with which she uses to seal: 't is my lady. To whom should this be?

FAB.   This wins him, liver and all.

MAL. [*Reads*]   Jove knows I love:
                                  But who?
                                  Lips, do not move;
                                  No man must know.

"No man must know." What follows? the numbers altered! "No man must know:" if this should be thee, Malvolio?

SIR TO.   Marry, hang thee, brock![10]

---

7. *employment*] work, business.

8. *gin*] snare.

9. *impressure her Lucrece*] the impression on the letter's sealing wax was made by a seal bearing the figure of the Roman matron Lucrece.

10. *brock*] badger.

MAL. [*Reads*] I may command where I adore;
        But silence, like a Lucrece knife,
        With bloodless stroke my heart doth gore:
        M, O, A, I, doth sway my life.

FAB. A fustian riddle!

SIR TO. Excellent wench, say I.

MAL. "M, O, A, I, doth sway my life." Nay, but first, let me see, let me see, let me see.

FAB. What dish o' poison has she dressed him!

SIR TO. And with what wing the staniel checks[11] at it!

MAL. "I may command where I adore." Why, she may command me: I serve her; she is my lady. Why, this is evident to any formal capacity;[12] there is no obstruction in this: and the end,—what should that alphabetical position portend? If I could make that resemble something in me,—Softly! M, O, A, I,—

SIR TO. O, ay, make up that: he is now at a cold scent.

FAB. Sowter will cry upon 't for all this, though it be as rank as a fox.[13]

MAL. M,—Malvolio; M,—why, that begins my name.

FAB. Did not I say he would work it out? the cur is excellent at faults.

MAL. M,—but then there is no consonancy in the sequel; that suffers under probation: A should follow, but O does.

FAB. And O shall end, I hope.

SIR TO. Ay, or I 'll cudgel him, and make him cry O!

MAL. And then I comes behind.

FAB. Ay, an you had any eye behind you, you might see more detraction at your heels than fortunes before you.

MAL. M, O, A, I; this simulation is not as the former: and yet, to crush this a little, it would bow to me, for every one of these letters are in my name. Soft! here follows prose.

[*Reads*] If this fall into thy hand, revolve. In my stars I am above thee; but be not afraid of greatness: some are born great, some achieve greatness, and some have greatness thrust upon 'em. Thy Fates open their hands; let thy blood and spirit embrace them; and, to inure thyself to what thou art like to be, cast thy humble slough and appear fresh. Be

---

11. *staniel checks*] staniel is a kind of hawk, and the verb "check" is a technical term in falconry, applied to the hawk's sudden swoop in flight when she catches sight of winged prey.

12. *formal capacity*] well-regulated mind.

13. *Sowter . . . fox*] "Sowter" (i. e., botcher, cobbler) is used as the name of a bad, dull hound. So poor a cur, although capable of any amount of bungling, must take this scent.

opposite with a kinsman, surly with servants; let thy tongue tang[14] arguments of state; put thyself into the trick of singularity: she thus advises thee that sighs for thee. Remember who commended thy yellow stockings, and wished to see thee ever cross-gartered:[15] I say, remember. Go to, thou art made, if thou desirest to be so; if not, let me see thee a steward still, the fellow of servants, and not worthy to touch Fortune's fingers. Farewell. She that would alter services with thee,

THE FORTUNATE-UNHAPPY.

Daylight and champain[16] discovers not more: this is open. I will be proud, I will read politic authors, I will baffle Sir Toby, I will wash off gross acquaintance, I will be point-devise[17] the very man. I do not now fool myself, to let imagination jade me; for every reason excites to this, that my lady loves me. She did commend my yellow stockings of late, she did praise my leg being cross-gartered; and in this she manifests herself to my love, and with a kind of injunction drives me to these habits of her liking. I thank my stars I am happy. I will be strange, stout, in yellow stockings, and crossgartered, even with the swiftness of putting on. Jove and my stars be praised! Here is yet a postscript.

[*Reads*] Thou canst not choose but know who I am. If thou entertainest my love, let it appear in thy smiling; thy smiles become thee well; therefore in my presence still smile, dear my sweet, I prithee.

Jove, I thank thee: I will smile; I will do every thing that thou wilt have me. [*Exit.*]

FAB. I will not give my part of this sport for a pension of thousands to be paid from the Sophy.[18]

SIR TO. I could marry this wench for this device,—

SIR AND. So could I too.

SIR TO. And ask no other dowry with her but such another jest.

SIR AND. Nor I neither.

FAB. Here comes my noble gull-catcher.[19]

Re-enter MARIA

---

14. *tang*] ring or sound loud with.
15. *yellow stockings and . . . cross-gartered*] Yellow was at the time a popular colour of stockings; men of fashion were in the habit of wearing their garters crossed both above and below the knee, with the ends fastened together behind the knee.
16. *champain*] open country.
17. *point-devise*] exactly (point-by-point) as the letter describes.
18. *the Sophy*] the Shah of Persia.
19. *gull-catcher*] fool-catcher.

SIR TO.   Wilt thou set thy foot o' my neck?

SIR AND.   Or o' mine either?

SIR TO.   Shall I play my freedom at tray-trip,[20] and become thy bond-slave?

SIR AND.   I' faith, or I either?

SIR TO.   Why, thou has put him in such a dream, that when the image of it leaves him he must run mad.

MAR.   Nay, but say true; does it work upon him?

SIR TO.   Like aqua-vitæ[21] with a midwife.

MAR.   If you will then see the fruits of the sport, mark his first approach before my lady: he will come to her in yellow stockings, and 't is a colour she abhors, and cross-gartered, a fashion she detests; and he will smile upon her, which will now be so unsuitable to her disposition, being addicted to a melancholy as she is, that it cannot but turn him into a notable contempt. If you will see it, follow me.

SIR TO.   To the gates of Tartar,[22] thou most excellent devil of wit!

SIR AND.   I 'll make one too.   [*Exeunt.*]

ACT III

SCENE I. OLIVIA'S *garden.*

Enter VIOLA, *and* Clown *with a tabor*

VIO.   Save thee, friend, and thy music: dost thou live by thy tabor?

CLO.   No, sir, I live by the church.

VIO.   Art thou a churchman?

CLO.   No such matter, sir: I do live by the church; for I do live at my house, and my house doth stand by the church.

VIO.   So thou mayst say, the king lies by a beggar, if a beggar dwell near him; or, the church stands by the tabor, if thy tabor stand by the church.

---

20. *tray-trip*] a game of dice in which rolling a three ("tray") was desirable.
21. *aqua-vitæ*] strong spirits.
22. *Tartar*] Hell.

CLO. You have said, sir. To see this age! A sentence[1] is but a cheveril[2] glove to a good wit: how quickly the wrong side may be turned outward!

VIO. Nay, that 's certain; they that dally nicely with words may quickly make them wanton.

CLO. I would, therefore, my sister had had no name, sir.

VIO. Why, man?

CLO. Why, sir, her name 's a word; and to dally with that word might make my sister wanton. But indeed words are very rascals since bonds disgraced them.

VIO. Thy reason, man?

CLO. Troth, sir, I can yield you none without words; and words are grown so false, I am loath to prove reason with them.

VIO. I warrant thou art a merry fellow and carest for nothing.

CLO. Not so, sir, I do care for something; but in my conscience, sir, I do not care for you: if that be to care for nothing, sir, I would it would make you invisible.

VIO. Art not thou the Lady Olivia's fool?

CLO. No, indeed, sir; the Lady Olivia has no folly: she will keep no fool, sir, till she be married; and fools are as like husbands as pilchards[3] are to herrings; the husband 's the bigger: I am indeed not her fool, but her corrupter of words.

VIO. I saw thee late at the Count Orsino's.

CLO. Foolery, sir, does walk about the orb like the sun, it shines every where. I would be sorry, sir, but the fool should be as oft with your master as with my mistress: I think I saw your wisdom there.

VIO. Nay, an thou pass upon me,[4] I 'll no more with thee. Hold, there 's expenses for thee.

CLO. Now Jove, in his next commodity of hair, send thee a beard!

VIO. By my troth, I 'll tell thee, I am almost sick for one; [*Aside*] though I would not have it grow on my chin. Is thy lady within?

CLO. Would not a pair of these have bred, sir?[5]

VIO. Yes, being kept together and put to use.

CLO. I would play Lord Pandarus of Phrygia, sir, to bring a Cressida to this Troilus.

---

1. *sentence*] maxim.
2. *cheveril*] very flexible leather from roebuck.
3. *pilchards*] or pilchers; fish resembling herrings.
4. *an . . . me*] if you make jokes at my expense.
5. *Would . . . bred*] Viola has given the clown two coins, and he wonders that they did not multiply (i.e., that his tip was not bigger).

VIO. I understand you, sir; 't is well begged.

CLO. The matter, I hope, is not great, sir, begging but a beggar: Cressida was a beggar. My lady is within, sir. I will construe to them whence you come; who you are and what you would are out of my welkin,[6] I might say "element," but the word is over-worn.

[*Exit.*]

VIO. This fellow is wise enough to play the fool;
And to do that well craves a kind of wit:
He must observe their mood on whom he jests,
The quality of persons, and the time,
And, like the haggard, check at every feather[7]
That comes before his eye. This is a practice
As full of labour as a wise man's art:
For folly that he wisely shows is fit;
But wise men, folly-fall'n, quite taint their wit.

Enter SIR TOBY, *and* SIR ANDREW

SIR TO. Save you, gentleman.

VIO. And you, sir.

SIR AND. Dieu vous garde, monsieur.

VIO. Et vous aussi; votre serviteur.[8]

SIR AND. I hope, sir, you are; and I am yours.

SIR TO. Will you encounter[9] the house? my niece is desirous you should enter, if your trade be to her.

VIO. I am bound to your niece, sir; I mean, she is the list[10] of my voyage.

SIR TO. Taste[11] your legs, sir; put them to motion.

VIO. My legs do better understand me, sir, than I understand what you mean by bidding me taste my legs.

SIR TO. I mean, to go, sir, to enter.

VIO. I will answer you with gait and entrance. But we are prevented.

Enter OLIVIA *and* MARIA

Most excellent accomplished lady, the heavens rain odours on you!

---

6. *welkin*] sky.
7. *like . . . feather*] see note 11 on page 32; a haggard is a wild, untrained hawk.
8. *Dieu . . . serviteur*] (Sir Andrew): God keep you, sir.
                 (Viola): And you, too; [I am] your servant.
9. *encounter*] enter.
10. *list*] bound, limit.
11. *Taste*] Try.

SIR AND.   That youth 's a rare courtier: "Rain odours"; well.

VIO.   My matter hath no voice, lady, but to your own most pregnant
and vouchsafed ear.

SIR AND.   "Odours," "pregnant," and "vouchsafed": I 'll get 'em all
three all ready.

OLI.   Let the garden door be shut, and leave me to my hearing.
[*Exeunt* SIR TOBY, SIR ANDREW, *and* MARIA.] Give me your hand,
sir.

VIO.   My duty, madam, and most humble service.

OLI.   What is your name?

VIO.   Cesario is your servant's name, fair princess.

OLI.   My servant, sir! 'T was never merry world
Since lowly feigning was call'd compliment:
You 're servant to the Count Orsino, youth.

VIO.   And he is yours, and his must needs be yours:
Your servant's servant is your servant, madam.

OLI.   For him, I think not on him: for his thoughts,
Would they were blanks, rather than fill'd with me!

VIO.   Madam, I come to whet your gentle thoughts
On his behalf.

OLI.   O, by your leave, I pray you;
I bade you never speak again of him:
But, would you undertake another suit,
I had rather hear you to solicit that
Than music from the spheres.

VIO.   Dear lady,—

OLI.   Give me leave, beseech you. I did send,
After the last enchantment you did here,
A ring in chase of you: so did I abuse
Myself, my servant and, I fear me, you:
Under your hard construction must I sit,
To force that on you, in a shameful cunning,
Which you knew none of yours: what might you think?
Have you not set mine honour at the stake
And baited it with all the unmuzzled thoughts
That tyrannous heart can think? To one of your receiving
Enough is shown: a cypress,[12] not a bosom,
Hides my heart. So, let me hear you speak.

---

12. *cypress*] mourning garments.

VIO.   I pity you.

OLI.   That 's a degree to love.

VIO.   No, not a grize;[13] for 't is a vulgar proof,
That very oft we pity enemies.

OLI.   Why, then, methinks, 't is time to smile again.
O world, how apt the poor are to be proud!
If one should be a prey, how much the better
To fall before the lion than the wolf!   [*Clock strikes.*]
The clock upbraids me with the waste of time.
Be not afraid, good youth, I will not have you:
And yet, when wit and youth is come to harvest,
Your wife is like to reap a proper man:
There lies your way, due west.

VIO.   Then westward-ho!
Grace and good disposition attend your ladyship!
You 'll nothing, madam, to my lord by me?

OLI.   Stay:
I prithee, tell me what thou think'st of me.

VIO.   That you do think you are not what you are.

OLI.   If I think so, I think the same of you.

VIO.   Then think you right: I am not what I am.

OLI.   I would you were as I would have you be!

VIO.   Would it be better, madam, than I am?
I wish it might, for now I am your fool.

OLI.   O, what a deal of scorn looks beautiful
In the contempt and anger of his lip!
A murderous guilt shows not itself more soon
Than love that would seem hid: love's night is noon.
Cesario, by the roses of the spring,
By maidenhood, honour, truth and every thing,
I love thee so, that, maugre[14] all thy pride,
Nor wit nor reason can my passion hide.
Do not extort thy reasons from this clause,
For that I woo, thou therefore hast no cause;
But rather reason thus with reason fetter,
Love sought is good, but given unsought is better.

VIO.   By innocence I swear, and by my youth,
I have one heart, one bosom and one truth,

---

13. *grize*] step.
14. *maugre*] in spite of.

And that no woman has; nor never none
Shall mistress be of it, save I alone.
And so adieu, good madam: never more
Will I my master's tears to you deplore.

OLI.   Yet come again; for thou perhaps mayst move
That heart, which now abhors, to like his love.   [*Exeunt.*]

SCENE II. OLIVIA'S *house.*

Enter SIR TOBY, SIR ANDREW, *and* FABIAN

SIR AND.   No, faith, I 'll not stay a jot longer.

SIR TO.   Thy reason, dear venom, give thy reason.

FAB.   You must needs yield your reason, Sir Andrew.

SIR AND.   Marry, I saw your niece do more favours to the count's serv-
      ing-man than ever she bestowed upon me; I saw 't i' the orchard.

SIR TO.   Did she see thee the while, old boy? tell me that.

SIR AND.   As plain as I see you now.

FAB.   This was a great argument of love in her toward you.

SIR AND.   'Slight, will you make an ass o' me?

FAB.   I will prove it legitimate, sir, upon the oaths of judgement and
      reason.

SIR TO.   And they have been grand-jurymen since before Noah was a
      sailor.

FAB.   She did show favour to the youth in your sight only to exasperate
      you, to awake your dormouse valour, to put fire in your heart, and
      brimstone in your liver. You should then have accosted her; and
      with some excellent jests, fire-new from the mint, you should have
      banged the youth into dumbness. This was looked for at your hand,
      and this was balked: the double gilt of this opportunity you let time
      wash off, and you are now sailed into the north of my lady's opin-
      ion; where you will hang like an icicle on a Dutchman's beard,[1]

---

1. *like an icicle . . . beard*] This simile seems to have been suggested by an English trans-
lation of a Dutch account of the discovery by a Dutchman, Willem Barents, in 1596,
of Nova Zembla, and of the explorer's sufferings from extremity of cold. The transla-
tion seems to have been first published in 1598, though no copy earlier than 1609 has
been met with.

unless you do redeem it by some laudable attempt either of valour or policy.

SIR AND.　An 't be any way, it must be with valour; for policy I hate: I had as lief be a Brownist[2] as a politician.

SIR TO.　Why, then, build me thy fortunes upon the basis of valour. Challenge me the count's youth to fight with him; hurt him in eleven places: my niece shall take note of it; and assure thyself, there is no love-broker in the world can more prevail in man's commendation with woman than report of valour.

FAB.　There is no way but this, Sir Andrew.

SIR AND.　Will either of you bear me a challenge to him?

SIR TO.　Go, write it in a martial hand; be curst[3] and brief; it is no matter how witty, so it be eloquent and full of invention: taunt him with the license of ink: if thou thou'st[4] him some thrice, it shall not be amiss; and as many lies as will lie in thy sheet of paper, although the sheet were big enough for the bed of Ware[5] in England, set 'em down: go, about it. Let there be gall enough in thy ink, though thou write with a goose-pen, no matter: about it.

SIR AND.　Where shall I find you?

SIR TO.　We 'll call thee at the cubiculo:[6] go.　　　[*Exit* SIR ANDREW.]

FAB.　This is a dear manakin to you, Sir Toby.

SIR TO.　I have been dear to him, lad, some two thousand strong, or so.

FAB.　We shall have a rare letter from him: but you 'll not deliver 't?

SIR TO.　Never trust me, then; and by all means stir on the youth to an answer. I think oxen and wainropes[7] cannot hale[8] them together. For Andrew, if he were opened, and you find so much blood in his liver as will clog the foot of a flea, I 'll eat the rest of the anatomy.

FAB.　And his opposite, the youth, bears in his visage no great presage of cruelty.

Enter MARIA

---

2. *Brownist*] a member of the religious sect of Puritan separatists or independents, which was founded by Robert Brown about 1580, and rapidly spread in secret, despite efforts made to suppress it.

3. *curst*] waspish, bellicose.

4. *thou thou'st*] To address a person as "thou" was held to be insulting.

5. *bed of Ware*] A giant bed, capable of holding twelve persons, long gave notoriety to an inn at Ware, a village in Hertfordshire.

6. *the cubiculo*] Sir Toby's bombastic periphrasis for Sir Andrew's lodging or bedroom.

7. *wainropes*] cart ropes.

8. *hale*] pull, drag.

SIR TO.   Look, where the youngest wren of nine comes.[9]

MAR.   If you desire the spleen, and will laugh yourselves into stitches,
follow me. Yond gull[10] Malvolio is turned heathen, a very renega-
do; for there is no Christian, that means to be saved by believing
rightly, can ever believe such impossible passages of grossness.[11]
He 's in yellow stockings.

SIR TO.   And cross-gartered?

MAR.   Most villanously; like a pedant that keeps a school i' the church.
I have dogged him, like his murderer. He does obey every point of
the letter that I dropped to betray him: he does smile his face into
more lines than is in the new map with the augmentation of the
Indies:[12] you have not seen such a thing as 't is. I can hardly forbear
hurling things at him. I know my lady will strike him: if she do,
he 'll smile and take 't for a great favour.

SIR TO.   Come, bring us, bring us where he is.   [*Exeunt.*]

SCENE III. *A street.*

Enter SEBASTIAN *and* ANTONIO

SEB.   I would not by my will have troubled you;
But, since you make your pleasure of your pains,
I will no further chide you.

ANT.   I could not stay behind you: my desire,
More sharp than filed steel, did spur me forth;
And not all love to see you, though so much
As might have drawn one to a longer voyage,
But jealousy what might befall your travel,
Being skilless in these parts; which to a stranger,
Unguided and unfriended, often prove

---

9. *wren of nine*] The allusion is to Maria's diminutive stature. The wren lays at a time
nine or ten eggs, usually of descending size.

10. *gull*] fool; someone easily tricked.

11. *passages of grossness*] acts of absurdity.

12. *new map . . . Indies*] A new map of the world was made in 1599 by Emmerie
Mollineux. It is multilineal, and plainly marks recent exploration in both the East and
the West hemispheres.

    Rough and unhospitable: my willing love,
    The rather by these arguments of fear,
    Set forth in your pursuit.

SEB.   My kind Antonio,
    I can no other answer make but thanks,
    And thanks; and ever. . . . oft good turns
    Are shuffled off with such uncurrent pay:
    But, were my worth as is my conscience firm,
    You should find better dealing. What 's to do?
    Shall we go see the reliques of this town?

ANT.   To-morrow, sir: best first go see your lodging.

SEB.   I am not weary, and 't is long to night:
    I pray you, let us satisfy our eyes
    With the memorials and the things of fame
    That do renown this city.

ANT.   Would you 'ld pardon me;
    I do not without danger walk these streets:
    Once, in a sea-fight, 'gainst the count his galleys
    I did some service; of such note indeed,
    That were I ta'en here it would scarce be answer'd.

SEB.   Belike you slew great number of his people.

ANT.   The offence is not of such a bloody nature;
    Albeit the quality of the time and quarrel
    Might well have given us bloody argument.
    It might have since been answer'd in repaying
    What we took from them; which, for traffic's sake,
    Most of our city did: only myself stood out;
    For which, if I be lapsed[1] in this place,
    I shall pay dear.

SEB.   Do not then walk too open.

ANT.   It doth not fit me. Hold, sir, here 's my purse.
    In the south suburbs, at the Elephant,[2]
    Is best to lodge: I will bespeak our diet,
    Whiles you beguile the time and feed your knowledge
    With viewing of the town: there shall you have me.

SEB.   Why I your purse?

ANT.   Haply your eye shall light upon some toy
    You have desire to purchase; and your store,

---

1. *lapsed*] caught, surprised.
2. *Elephant*] an inn.

I think, is not for idle markets, sir.

SEB. I 'll be your purse-bearer and leave you
       For an hour.

ANT.   To the Elephant.

SEB.   I do remember.   [*Exeunt.*]

SCENE IV. OLIVIA'S *garden.*

Enter OLIVIA *and* MARIA

OLI. I have sent after him: he[1] says he 'll come;
       How shall I feast him? what bestow of him?
       For youth is bought more oft than begg'd or borrow'd.
       I speak too loud.
       Where is Malvolio? he is sad and civil,
       And suits well for a servant with my fortunes:
       Where is Malvolio?

MAR. He 's coming, madam; but in very strange manner. He is, sure,
       possessed, madam.

OLI. Why, what 's the matter? does he rave?

MAR. No, madam, he does nothing but smile: your ladyship were
       best to have some guard about you, if he come; for, sure, the man
       is tainted in 's wits.

OLI. Go call him hither. [*Exit* MARIA.] I am as mad as he,
       If sad and merry madness equal be.

Re-enter MARIA, *with* MALVOLIO

       How now, Malvolio!

MAL. Sweet lady, ho, ho.

OLI. Smilest thou?
       I sent for thee upon a sad occasion.

MAL. Sad, lady? I could be sad: this does make some obstruction in
       the blood, this cross-gartering; but what of that? if it please the eye
       of one, it is with me as the very true sonnet is, "Please one, and
       please all."

---

1. *he*] Cesario (i.e., Viola).

OLI. Why, how dost thou, man? what is the matter with thee?

MAL. Not black in my mind, though yellow in my legs. It did come to his hands, and commands shall be executed: I think we do know the sweet Roman hand.

OLI. Wilt thou go to bed, Malvolio?

MAL. To bed! ay, sweet-heart, and I 'll come to thee.

OLI. God comfort thee! Why dost thou smile so and kiss thy hand so oft?

MAR. How do you, Malvolio?

MAL. At your request! yes; nightingales answer daws.

MAR. Why appear you with this ridiculous boldness before my lady?

MAL. "Be not afraid of greatness": 't was well writ.

OLI. What meanest thou by that, Malvolio?

MAL. "Some are born great,"—

OLI. Ha!

MAL. "Some achieve greatness,"—

OLI. What sayest thou?

MAL. "And some have greatness thrust upon them."

OLI. Heaven restore thee!

MAL. "Remember who commended thy yellow stockings,"—

OLI. Thy yellow stockings!

MAL. "And wished to see thee cross-gartered."

OLI. Cross-gartered!

MAL. "Go to, thou art made, if thou desirest to be so";—

OLI. Am I made?

MAL. "If not, let me see thee a servant still."

OLI. Why, this is very midsummer madness.

Enter Servant

SER. Madam, the young gentleman of the Count Orsino's is returned: I could hardly entreat him back: he attends your ladyship's pleasure.

OLI. I 'll come to him. [*Exit* Servant.] Good Maria, let this fellow be looked to. Where 's my cousin Toby? Let some of my people have a special care of him: I would not have him miscarry for the half of my dowry. [*Exeunt* OLIVIA *and* MARIA.]

MAL. O, ho! do you come near² me now? no worse man than Sir Toby to look to me! This concurs directly with the letter: she sends

---

2. *come near*] understand.

him on purpose, that I may appear stubborn to him; for she incites me to that in the letter. "Cast thy humble slough," says she; "be opposite with a kinsman, surly with servants; let thy tongue tang with arguments of state; put thyself into the trick of singularity"; and consequently sets down the manner how; as, a sad face, a reverend carriage, a slow tongue, in the habit of some sir of note, and so forth. I have limed³ her; but it is Jove's doing, and Jove make me thankful! And when she went away now, "Let this fellow be looked to": fellow! not Malvolio, nor after my degree, but fellow. Why, every thing adheres together, that no dram of a scruple, no scruple of a scruple, no obstacle, no incredulous or unsafe circumstance— What can be said? Nothing that can be can come between me and the full prospect of my hopes. Well, Jove, not I, is the doer of this, and he is to be thanked.

Re-enter MARIA, *with* SIR TOBY *and* FABIAN

SIR TO. Which way is he, in the name of sanctity? If all the devils of hell be drawn in little, and Legion⁴ himself possessed him, yet I 'll speak to him.

FAB. Here he is, here he is. How is 't with you, sir? how is 't with you, man?

MAL. Go off; I discard you: let me enjoy my private: go off.

MAR. Lo, how hollow the fiend speaks within him! did not I tell you? Sir Toby, my lady prays you to have a care of him.

MAL. Ah, ha! does she so?

SIR TO. Go to, go to; peace, peace; we must deal gently with him: let me alone. How do you, Malvolio? how is 't with you? What, man! defy the devil: consider, he 's an enemy to mankind.

MAL. Do you know what you say?

MAR. La you, an you speak ill of the devil, how he takes it at heart! Pray God, he be not bewitched!

FAB. Carry his water to the wise woman.

MAR. Marry, and it shall be done to-morrow morning, if I live. My lady would not lose him for more than I 'll say.

MAL. How now, mistress!

MAR. O Lord!

---

3. *limed*] caught, ensnared.
4. *Legion*] in the New Testament Christ exorcises a demon who calls himself "Legion: for we are many" (Mark 5:9).

SIR TO. Prithee, hold thy peace; this is not the way: do you not see
　　　you move him? let me alone with him.
FAB. No way but gentleness; gently, gently: the fiend is rough, and
　　　will not be roughly used.
SIR TO. Why, how now, my bawcock! how dost thou, chuck?
MAL. Sir!
SIR TO. Ay, Biddy,[5] come with me. What, man! 't is not for gravity to
　　　play at cherry-pit with Satan: hang him, foul collier![6]
MAR. Get him to say his prayers, good Sir Toby, get him to pray.
MAL. My prayers, minx!
MAR. No, I warrant you, he will not hear of godliness.
MAL. Go, hang yourselves all! you are idle shallow things: I am not of
　　　your element: you shall know more hereafter.　　　　　　[*Exit.*]
SIR TO. Is 't possible?
FAB. If this were played upon a stage now, I could condemn it as an
　　　improbable fiction.
SIR TO. His very genius hath taken the infection of the device, man.
MAR. Nay, pursue him now, lest the device take air and taint.
FAB. Why, we shall make him mad indeed.
MAR. The house will be the quieter.
SIR TO. Come, we 'll have him in a dark room and bound. My niece
　　　is already in the belief that he 's mad: we may carry it thus, for our
　　　pleasure and his penance, till our very pastime, tired out of breath,
　　　prompt us to have mercy on him: at which time we will bring the
　　　device to the bar and crown thee for a finder of madmen.[7] But see,
　　　but see.

Enter SIR ANDREW

FAB. More matter for a May morning.[8]
SIR AND. Here 's the challenge, read it: I warrant there 's vinegar and
　　　pepper in 't.
FAB. Is 't so saucy?
SIR AND. Ay, is 't, I warrant him: do but read.

---

5. *Biddy*] term used to call chickens.
6. *play . . . collier!*] cherry-pit was a children's game played by throwing cherry pits into a
little hole; the references to Satan and the collier allude to the proverb "Like will to
like, as the devil with the collier," a digger or seller of coals.
7. *finder of madmen*] those appointed to report on persons suspected of madness.
8. *More . . . morning*] On May Day it was the custom to perform comic interludes or fan-
tastic dances.

SIR. TO.   Give me. [*Reads*] Youth, whatsoever thou art, thou art but a
scurvy fellow.

FAB.   Good, and valiant.

SIR TO.   [*Reads*] Wonder not, nor admire not in thy mind, why I do call
thee so, for I will show thee no reason for 't.

FAB.   A good note; that keeps you from the blow of the law.

SIR TO.   [*Reads*] Thou comest to the lady Olivia, and in my sight she uses
thee kindly: but thou liest in thy throat; that is not the matter I challenge
thee for.

FAB.   Very brief, and to exceeding good sense—less.

SIR TO.   [*Reads*] I will waylay thee going home; where if it be thy chance
to kill me,—

FAB.   Good.

SIR TO.   [*Reads*] Thou killest me like a rogue and a villain.

FAB.   Still you keep o' the windy side of the law: good.

SIR TO.   [*Reads*] Fare thee well; and God have mercy upon one of our
souls! He may have mercy upon mine; but my hope is better, and so look
to thyself. Thy friend, as thou usest him, and thy sworn enemy,

ANDREW AGUECHEEK.

If this letter move him not, his legs cannot: I 'll give 't him.

MAR.   You may have very fit occasion for 't: he is now in some com-
merce with my lady, and will by and by depart.

SIR TO.   Go, Sir Andrew; scout me for him at the corner of the
orchard like a bum-baily:[9] so soon as ever thou seest him, draw;
and, as thou drawest, swear horrible; for it comes to pass oft that a
terrible oath, with a swaggering accent sharply twanged off, gives
manhood more approbation than ever proof itself would have
earned him. Away!

SIR AND.   Nay, let me alone for swearing.   [*Exit.*]

SIR TO.   Now will not I deliver his letter: for the behaviour of the
young gentleman gives him out to be of good capacity and breeding; his employment between his lord and my niece confirms no
less: therefore this letter, being so excellently ignorant, will breed
no terror in the youth: he will find it comes from a clodpole. But,
sir, I will deliver his challenge by word of mouth; set upon
Aguecheek a notable report of valour; and drive the gentleman, as
I know his youth will aptly receive it, into a most hideous opinion

---

9. *bum-baily*] junior officer employed in making arrests.

of his rage, skill, fury, and impetuosity. This will so fright them
both, that they will kill one another by the look, like cockatrices.[10]

Re-enter OLIVIA, *with* VIOLA

FAB. Here he comes with your niece: give them way till he take leave,
and presently after him.

SIR TO. I will meditate the while upon some horrid message for a
challenge.   [*Exeunt* SIR TOBY, FABIAN, *and* MARIA.]

OLI. I have said too much unto a heart of stone,
And laid mine honour too unchary out:
There 's something in me that reproves my fault;
But such a headstrong potent fault it is,
That it but mocks reproof.

VIO. With the same 'haviour that your passion bears
Goes on my master's grief.

OLI. Here, wear this jewel for me, 't is my picture;
Refuse it not; it hath no tongue to vex you;
And I beseech you come again to-morrow.
What shall you ask of me that I 'll deny,
That honour saved may upon asking give?

VIO. Nothing but this;—your true love for my master.

OLI. How with mine honour may I give him that
Which I have given to you?

VIO.   I will acquit you.

OLI. Well, come again to-morrow: fare thee well:
A fiend like thee might bear my soul to hell.   [*Exit.*]

Re-enter SIR TOBY *and* FABIAN

SIR TO. Gentleman, God save thee.

VIO. And you, sir.

SIR TO. That defence thou hast, betake thee to 't: of what nature the
wrongs are thou hast done him, I know not; but thy intercepter,
full of despite, bloody as the hunter, attends thee at the orchard-
end: dismount thy tuck,[11] be yare[12] in thy preparation, for thy
assailant is quick, skilful and deadly.

VIO. You mistake, sir; I am sure no man hath any quarrel to me: my

---

10. *cockatrices*] imaginary birds, supposed to be hatched from cocks' eggs, and that could
kill with a look.

11. *dismount thy tuck*] draw thy sword or rapier.

12. *yare*] ready, brisk.

remembrance is very free and clear from any image of offence done to any man.

SIR TO.   You 'll find it otherwise, I assure you: therefore, if you hold your life at any price, betake you to your guard; for your opposite hath in him what youth, strength, skill and wrath can furnish man withal.

VIO.   I pray you, sir, what is he?

SIR TO.   He is knight, dubbed with unhatched rapier and on carpet consideration;[13] but he is a devil in private brawl: souls and bodies hath he divorced three; and his incensement at this moment is so implacable, that satisfaction can be none but by pangs of death and sepulchre. Hob, nob,[14] is his word; give 't or take 't.

VIO.   I will return again into the house and desire some conduct of the lady. I am no fighter. I have heard of some kind of men that put quarrels purposely on others, to taste their valour: belike this is a man of that quirk.

SIR TO.   Sir, no; his indignation derives itself out of a very competent injury: therefore, get you on and give him his desire. Back you shall not to the house, unless you undertake that with me which with as much safety you might answer him: therefore, on, or strip your sword stark naked; for meddle you must, that 's certain, or forswear to wear iron about you.

VIO.   This is as uncivil as strange. I beseech you, do me this courteous office, as to know of the knight what my offence to him is: it is something of my negligence, nothing of my purpose.

SIR TO.   I will do so. Signior Fabian, stay you by this gentleman till my return.   [Exit.]

VIO.   Pray you, sir, do you know of this matter?

FAB.   I know the knight is incensed against you, even to a mortal arbitrement;[15] but nothing of the circumstance more.

VIO.   I beseech you, what manner of man is he?

FAB.   Nothing of that wonderful promise, to read him by his form, as you are like to find him in the proof of his valour. He is, indeed, sir, the most skilful, bloody and fatal opposite that you could pos-

---

13. *knight . . . on carpet consideration*] a carpet knight was one whose title was not derived from military service; an "unhatched rapier" is a rapier that has not been used in military combat.

14. *Hob, nob*] "Hob" is a corruption of "have," and the expression here means "have or have not," "hit or miss."

15. *arbitrement*] decision.

sibly have found in any part of Illyria. Will you walk towards him?
I will make your peace with him if I can.

VIO.　I shall be much bound to you for 't: I am one that had rather go
with sir priest than sir knight: I care not who knows so much of my
mettle.　　　　　　　　　　　　　　　　　　　　　　　[*Exeunt.*]

Re-enter SIR TOBY, *with* SIR ANDREW

SIR TO.　Why, man, he 's a very devil; I have not seen such a firago.[16]
I had a pass with him, rapier, scabbard and all, and he gives me
the stuck in[17] with such a mortal motion, that it is inevitable; and
on the answer, he pays you as surely as your feet hit the ground
they step on. They say he has been fencer to the Sophy.

SIR AND.　Pox on 't, I 'll not meddle with him.

SIR TO.　Ay, but he will not now be pacified: Fabian can scarce hold
him yonder.

SIR AND.　Plague on 't, an I thought he had been valiant and so cunning in fence, I 'ld have seen him damned ere I 'ld have chal-
lenged him. Let him let the matter slip, and I 'll give him my
horse, grey Capilet.[18]

SIR TO.　I 'll make the motion: stand here, make a good show on 't:
this shall end without the perdition of souls. [*Aside*] Marry, I 'll
ride your horse as well as I ride you.

Re-enter FABIAN *and* VIOLA

[*To* FAB.] I have his horse to take up the quarrel: I have persuaded him
the youth 's a devil.

FAB.　He is as horribly conceited of him; and pants and looks pale, as
if a bear were at his heels.

SIR TO.　[*To* VIO.] There's no remedy, sir; he will fight with you for 's
oath sake: marry, he hath better bethought him of his quarrel, and
he finds that now scarce to be worth talking of: therefore draw, for
the supportance of his vow; he protests he will not hurt you.

VIO.　[*Aside*] Pray God defend me! A little thing would make me tell
them how much I lack of a man.

FAB.　Give ground, if you see him furious.

SIR TO.　Come, Sir Andrew, there 's no remedy; the gentleman will,
for his honour's sake, have one bout with you; he cannot by the

16. *firago*] virago.
17. *stuck in*] Sir Toby's corruption of the Italian fencing term for thrust, "stoccata."
18. *Capilet*] apparently a diminutive, formed from "capul" or "caple," a north-country
word for a horse.

duello[19] avoid it: but he has promised me, as he is a gentleman and
a soldier, he will not hurt you. Come on; to 't.

SIR AND.   Pray God, he keep his oath!

VIO.   I do assure you, 't is against my will.   [*They draw.*]

Enter Antonio

ANT.   Put up your sword. If this young gentleman
        Have done offence, I take the fault on me:
        If you offend him, I for him defy you.

SIR TO.   You, sir! why, what are you?

ANT.   One, sir, that for his love dares yet do more
        Than you have heard him brag to you he will.

SIR TO.   Nay, if you be an undertaker,[20] I am for you.   [*They draw.*]

Enter Officers

FAB.   O good Sir Toby, hold! here comes the officers.

SIR TO.   I 'll be with you anon.

VIO.   Pray, sir, put your sword up, if you please.

SIR AND.   Marry, will I, sir; and, for that I promised you, I 'll be as
good as my word: he will bear you easily and reins well.[21]

FIRST OFF.   This is the man; do thy office.

SEC. OFF.   Antonio, I arrest thee at the suit of Count Orsino.

ANT.   You do mistake me, sir.

FIRST OFF.   No, sir, no jot; I know your favour well,
        Though now you have no sea-cap on your head.
        Take him away: he knows I know him well.

ANT.   I must obey. [*To* VIO.] This comes with seeking you:
        But there 's no remedy; I shall answer it.
        What will you do, now my necessity
        Makes me to ask you for my purse? It grieves me
        Much more for what I cannot do for you
        Than what befalls myself. You stand amazed;
        But be of comfort.

SEC. OFF.   Come, sir, away.

ANT.   I must entreat of you some of that money.

VIO.   What money, sir?
        For the fair kindness you have show'd me here,

---

19. *duello*] the code of the duel.
20. *undertaker*] an intermedler.
21. *he . . . well*] Sir Andrew refers to his horse.

And, part, being prompted by your present trouble,
Out of my lean and low ability
I 'll lend you something: my having[22] is not much;
I 'll make division of my present[23] with you:
Hold, there 's half my coffer.

ANT.   Will you deny me now?
Is 't possible that my deserts to you
Can lack persuasion? Do not tempt my misery,
Lest that it make me so unsound a man
As to upbraid you with those kindnesses
That I have done for you.

VIO.   I know of none;
Nor know I you by voice or any feature:
I hate ingratitude more in a man
Than lying vainness,[24] babbling drunkenness,
Or any taint of vice whose strong corruption
Inhabits our frail blood.

ANT.   O heavens themselves!
SEC. OFF.   Come, sir, I pray you, go.
ANT.   Let me speak a little. This youth that you see here
I snatch'd one half out of the jaws of death;
Relieved him with such sanctity of love;
And to his image, which methought did promise
Most venerable worth, did I devotion.
FIRST OFF.   What 's that to us? The time goes by: away!
ANT.   But O how vile an idol proves his god!
Thou hast, Sebastian, done good feature shame.
In nature there 's no blemish but the mind;
None can be call'd deform'd but the unkind:
Virtue is beauty; but the beauteous evil
Are empty trunks, o'erflourish'd by the devil.
FIRST OFF.   The man grows mad: away with him! Come, come, sir.
ANT.   Lead me on.   [*Exit with* Officers.]
VIO.   Methinks his words do from such passion fly,
That he believes himself: so do not I.
Prove true, imagination, O prove true,
That I, dear brother, be now ta'en for you!

---

22. *having*] property, fortune.
23. *my present*] my present store.
24. *lying vainness*] lying boastfulness.

SIR TO.   Come hither, knight; come hither, Fabian: we 'll whisper
          o'er a couplet or two of most sage saws.
VIO.   He named Sebastian: I my brother know
       Yet living in my glass; even such and so
       In favour was my brother, and he went
       Still in this fashion, colour, ornament,
       For him I imitate: O, if it prove,
       Tempests are kind and salt waves fresh in love!   [*Exit.*]
SIR TO.   A very dishonest paltry boy, and more a coward than a hare:
          his dishonesty appears in leaving his friend here in necessity and
          denying him; and for his cowardship, ask Fabian.
FAB.   A coward, a most devout coward, religious in it.
SIR AND.   'Slid,[25] I 'll after him again and beat him.
SIR TO.   Do; cuff him soundly, but never draw thy sword.
SIR AND.   An I do not,—   [*Exit.*]
FAB.   Come, let 's see the event.
SIR TO.   I dare lay any money 't will be nothing yet.   [*Exeunt.*]

ACT IV

SCENE I. *Before* OLIVIA'S *house.*

Enter SEBASTIAN *and* Clown

CLO.   Will you make me believe that I am not sent for you?
SEB.   Go to, go to, thou art a foolish fellow:
       Let me be clear of thee.
CLO.   Well held out, i' faith! No, I do not know you; nor I am not sent
       to you by my lady, to bid you come speak with her; nor your name
       is not Master Cesario; nor this is not my nose neither. Nothing
       that is so is so.
SEB.   I prithee, vent thy folly somewhere else:
       Thou know'st not me.
CLO.   Vent my folly! he has heard that word of some great man and
       now applies it to a fool. Vent my folly! I am afraid this great lub-

---

25. *'Slid*] an oath, from "God's [eye]lid."

ber, the world, will prove a cockney.[1] I prithee now, ungird thy strangeness and tell me what I shall vent to my lady: shall I vent to her that thou art coming?

SEB.   I prithee, foolish Greek,[2] depart from me:
    There 's money for thee: if you tarry longer,
    I shall give worse payment.

CLO.   By my troth, thou hast an open hand. These wise men that give fools money get themselves a good report—after fourteen years' purchase.

Enter SIR ANDREW, SIR TOBY, *and* FABIAN

SIR AND.   Now, sir, have I met you again? there 's for you.

SEB.   Why, there 's for thee, and there, and there.
    Are all the people mad?

SIR TO.   Hold, sir, or I 'll throw your dagger o'er the house.

CLO.   This will I tell my lady straight: I would not be in some of your coats for two pence.   [*Exit.*]

SIR TO.   Come on, sir; hold.

SIR AND.   Nay, let him alone: I 'll go another way to work with him; I 'll have an action of battery against him, if there be any law in Illyria: though I struck him first, yet it 's no matter for that.

SEB.   Let go thy hand.

SIR TO.   Come, sir, I will not let you go. Come, my young soldier, put up your iron: you are well fleshed; come on.

SEB.   I will be free from thee. What wouldst thou now?
    If thou darest tempt me further, draw thy sword.

SIR TO.   What, what? Nay, then I must have an ounce or two of this malapert blood from you.

Enter OLIVIA

OLI.   Hold, Toby; on thy life, I charge thee, hold!

SIR TO.   Madam!

OLI.   Will it be ever thus? Ungracious wretch,
    Fit for the mountains and the barbarous caves,
    Where manners ne'er were preach'd! out of my sight!
    Be not offended, dear Cesario.
    Rudesby,[3] be gone! [*Exeunt* SIR TOBY, SIR ANDREW, *and* FABIAN.]
                I prithee, gentle friend,

---

1. *cockney*] an effeminate fellow.
2. *Greek*] colloquial term for "fellow" or "companion."
3. *Rudesby*] boor.

Let thy fair wisdom, not thy passion, sway
In this uncivil and unjust extent
Against thy peace. Go with me to my house;
And hear thou there how many fruitless pranks
This ruffian hath botch'd up, that thou thereby
Mayst smile at this: thou shalt not choose but go:
Do not deny. Beshrew his soul for me,
He started one poor heart of mine in thee.

SEB.   What relish is in this? how runs the stream?
Or I am mad, or else this is a dream:
Let fancy still my sense in Lethe steep;
If it be thus to dream, still let me sleep!

OLI.   Nay, come, I prithee: would thou 'ldst be ruled by me!

SEB.   Madam, I will.

OLI.   O, say so, and so be!   [*Exeunt.*]

SCENE II. OLIVIA'S *house*.

Enter MARIA *and* Clown

MAR.   Nay, I prithee, put on this gown and this beard; make him
    believe thou art Sir Topas the curate: do it quickly; I 'll call Sir
    Toby the whilst.   [*Exit.*]

CLO.   Well, I 'll put it on, and I will dissemble myself in 't; and I
    would I were the first that ever dissembled in such a gown. I am
    not tall enough to become the function well, nor lean enough to
    be thought a good student; but to be said an honest man and a
    good housekeeper goes as fairly as to say a careful man and a great
    scholar. The competitors enter.

Enter SIR TOBY *and* MARIA

SIR TO.   Jove bless thee, master Parson.

CLO.   Bonos dies, Sir Toby: for, as the old hermit of Prague, that never
    saw pen and ink, very wittily said to a niece of King Gorboduc,[1]
    "That that is is"; so I, being master Parson, am master Parson; for,
    what is "that" but "that," and "is" but "is"?

----
1. *Gorboduc*] a king of ancient Britain..

SIR TO. To him, Sir Topas.

CLO. What, ho, I say! peace in this prison!

SIR TO. The knave counterfeits well; a good knave.

MAL. [*within*] Who calls there?

CLO. Sir Topas the curate, who comes to visit Malvolio the lunatic.

MAL. Sir Topas, Sir Topas, good Sir Topas, go to my lady.

CLO. Out, hyperbolical fiend! how vexest thou this man! talkest thou nothing but of ladies?

SIR TO. Well said, master Parson.

MAL. Sir Topas, never was man thus wronged: good Sir Topas, do not think I am mad: they have laid me here in hideous darkness.

CLO. Fie, thou dishonest Satan! I call thee by the most modest terms; for I am one of those gentle ones that will use the devil himself with courtesy: sayest thou that house is dark?

MAL. As hell, Sir Topas.

CLO. Why, it hath bay windows transparent as barricadoes, and the clearstories² toward the south north are as lustrous as ebony; and yet complainest thou of obstruction?

MAL. I am not mad, Sir Topas: I say to you, this house is dark.

CLO. Madman, thou errest: I say, there is no darkness but ignorance; in which thou art more puzzled than the Egyptians in their fog.³

MAL. I say, this house is as dark as ignorance, though ignorance were as dark as hell; and I say, there was never man thus abused. I am no more mad than you are: make the trial of it any constant question.

CLO. What is the opinion of Pythagoras concerning wild fowl?

MAL. That the soul of our grandam might haply inhabit a bird.

CLO. What thinkest thou of his opinion?

MAL. I think nobly of the soul, and no way approve his opinion.

CLO. Fare thee well. Remain thou still in darkness: thou shalt hold the opinion of Pythagoras ere I will allow of thy wits; and fear to kill a woodcock, lest thou dispossess the soul of thy grandam. Fare thee well.

MAL. Sir Topas, Sir Topas!

SIR TO. My most exquisite Sir Topas!

CLO. Nay, I am for all waters.

MAR. Thou mightst have done this without thy beard and gown: he sees thee not.

---

2. *clearstories*] according to some sources, the upper row of windows on a house or church.

3. *Egyptians . . . fog*] One of the seven plagues inflicted upon the Egyptians as God's punishment of the Pharaoh for refusing to free the Hebrew slaves (see Exodus 10:21–23).

SIR TO.   To him in thine own voice, and bring me word how thou findest him: I would we were well rid of this knavery. If he may be conveniently delivered, I would he were; for I am now so far in offence with my niece, that I cannot pursue with any safety this sport to the upshot. Come by and by to my chamber.

                                        [*Exeunt* SIR TOBY *and* MARIA.]

CLO.   [*Singing*] Hey, Robin, jolly Robin,
                     Tell me how thy lady does.

MAL.   Fool,—

CLO.   My lady is unkind, perdy.[4]

MAL.   Fool,—

CLO.   Alas, why is she so?

MAL.   Fool, I say,—

CLO.   She loves another—Who calls, ha?

MAL.   Good fool, as ever thou wilt deserve well at my hand, help me to a candle, and pen, ink and paper: as I am a gentleman, I will live to be thankful to thee for 't.

CLO.   Master Malvolio!

MAL.   Ay, good fool.

CLO.   Alas, sir, how fell you besides your five wits?[5]

MAL.   Fool, there was never man so notoriously abused: I am as well in my wits, fool, as thou art.

CLO.   But as well? then you are mad indeed, if you be no better in your wits than a fool.

MAL.   They have here propertied me;[6] keep me in darkness, send ministers to me, asses, and do all they can to face me out of my wits.

CLO.   Advise you what you say; the minister is here. Malvolio, Malvolio, thy wits the heavens restore! endeavour thyself to sleep, and leave thy vain bibble babble.

MAL.   Sir Topas,—

CLO.   Maintain no words with him, good fellow. Who, I, sir? not I, sir. God be wi' you, good Sir Topas. Marry, amen. I will, sir, I will.

MAL.   Fool, fool, fool, I say,—

CLO.   Alas, sir, be patient. What say you, sir? I am shent[7] for speaking to you.

---

4. *perdy*] "by God" (from "par Dieu").
5. *five wits*] The "five wits" were common wit or intellectual power, imagination, fancy, estimation and memory.
6. *propertied*] as a verb, to make property of, to make a tool, prop of.
7. *shent*] blamed, reproached.

MAL. Good fool, help me to some light and some paper: I tell thee, I
am as well in my wits as any man in Illyria.

CLO. Well-a-day that you were, sir!

MAL. By this hand, I am. Good fool, some ink, paper and light; and
convey what I will set down to my lady. It shall advantage thee
more than ever the bearing of letter did.

CLO. I will help you to 't. But tell me true, are you not mad indeed?
or do you but counterfeit?

MAL. Believe me, I am not; I tell thee true.

CLO. Nay, I 'll ne'er believe a madman till I see his brains. I will fetch
you light and paper and ink.

MAL. Fool, I 'll requite it in the highest degree: I prithee, be gone.

CLO. [*Singing*] I am gone, sir,
              And anon, sir,
      I 'll be with you again,
            In a trice,
            Like to the old vice,
      Your need to sustain;
      Who, with dagger of lath,[8]
      In his rage and his wrath,
            Cries, ah, ha! to the devil:
      Like a mad lad,
      Pare thy nails, dad;
      Adieu, goodman devil.   [*Exit.*]

SCENE III. OLIVIA'S *garden.*

Enter SEBASTIAN

SEB. This is the air; that is the glorious sun;
This pearl she gave me, I do feel 't and see 't;
And though 't is wonder that enwraps me thus,
Yet 't is not madness. Where 's Antonio, then?
I could not find him at the Elephant:
Yet there he was; and there I found this credit,[1]

---

8. *lath*] a piece of wood.

1. *credit*] belief or opinion.

That he did range the town to seek me out.
His counsel now might do me golden service;
For though my soul disputes well with my sense,
That this may be some error, but no madness,
Yet doth this accident and flood of fortune
So far exceed all instance, all discourse,
That I am ready to distrust mine eyes
And wrangle with my reason, that persuades me
To any other trust but that I am mad,
Or else the lady's mad; yet, if 't were so,
She could not sway her house, command her followers,
Take and give back affairs and their dispatch
With such a smooth, discreet, and stable bearing
As I perceive she does: there 's something in 't
That is deceivable. But here the lady comes.

Enter OLIVIA *and* Priest

OLI.   Blame not this haste of mine. If you mean well,
       Now go with me and with this holy man
       Into the chantry by: there, before him,
       And underneath that consecrated roof,
       Plight me the full assurance of your faith;
       That my most jealous and too doubtful soul
       May live at peace. He shall conceal it
       Whiles you are willing it shall come to note,
       What time we will our celebration keep
       According to my birth. What do you say?
SEB.   I 'll follow this good man, and go with you;
       And, having sworn truth, ever will be true.
OLI.   Then lead the way, good father; and heavens so shine,
       That they may fairly note this act of mine!   [*Exeunt.*]

ACT V

SCENE I. *Before* OLIVIA'S *house.*

Enter Clown *and* FABIAN

FAB. Now, as thou lovest me, let me see his letter.

CLO. Good Master Fabian, grant me another request.

FAB. Any thing.

CLO. Do not desire to see this letter.

FAB. This is, to give a dog, and in recompense desire my dog again.

Enter DUKE, VIOLA, CURIO, *and* Lords

DUKE. Belong you to the Lady Olivia, friends?

CLO. Ay, sir; we are some of her trappings.

DUKE. I know thee well: how dost thou, my good fellow?

CLO. Truly, sir, the better for my foes and the worse for my friends.

DUKE. Just the contrary; the better for thy friends.

CLO. No, sir, the worse.

DUKE. How can that be?

CLO. Marry, sir, they praise me and make an ass of me; now my foes tell me plainly I am an ass: so that by my foes, sir, I profit in the knowledge of myself; and by my friends I am abused: so that, conclusions to be as kisses, if your four negatives make your two affirmatives, why then, the worse for my friends, and the better for my foes.

DUKE. Why, this is excellent.

CLO. By my troth, sir, no; though it please you to be one of my friends.

DUKE. Thou shalt not be the worse for me: there's gold.

CLO. But that it would be double-dealing, sir, I would you could make it another.

DUKE. O, you give me ill counsel.

CLO. Put your grace in your pocket, sir, for this once, and let your flesh and blood obey it.

DUKE. Well, I will be so much a sinner, to be a double-dealer: there's another.

CLO. Primo, secundo, tertio, is a good play; and the old saying is, the

third pays for all: the triplex, sir, is a good tripping measure; or the
bells of Saint Bennet,[1] sir, may put you in mind; one, two, three.

DUKE.   You can fool no more money out of·me at this throw: if you
will let your lady know I am here to speak with her, and bring her
along with you, it may awake my bounty further.

CLO.   Marry, sir, lullaby to your bounty till I come again. I go, sir; but
I would not have you to think that my desire of having is the sin
of covetousness: but, as you say, sir, let your bounty take a nap, I
will awake it anon.   [Exit.]

VIO.   Here comes the man, sir, that did rescue me.

Enter ANTONIO *and* Officers

DUKE.   That face of his I do remember well;
Yet, when I saw it last, it was besmear'd
As black as Vulcan[2] in the smoke of war:
A bawbling[3] vessel was he captain of,
For shallow draught and bulk unprizable;[4]
With which such scathful grapple did he make
With the most noble bottom of our fleet,
That very envy and the tongue of loss
Cried fame and honour on him.[5] What 's the matter?

FIRST OFF.   Orsino, this is that Antonio
That took the Phœnix and her fraught[6] from Candy;[7]
And this is he that did the Tiger board,
When your young nephew Titus lost his leg:
Here in the streets, desperate of shame and state,[8]
In private brabble did we apprehend him.

VIO.   He did me kindness, sir, drew on my side;
But in conclusion put strange speech upon me:
I know not what 't was but distraction.

---

1. *bells of Saint Bennet*] a reference to the chimes sounded by the bells of St. Bennet's
Church on Paul's Wharf, which was destroyed in the great fire of London.

2. *Vulcan*] the Roman god of fire and metalsmithing, usually portrayed with skin black-
ened from the smoke of his forge

3. *bawbling*] trifling, of small value.

4. *unprizable*] without value as a prize of war.

5. *scathful grapple . . . on him*] He grappled with such destructive violence with the finest
ship of our fleet that those who had had best right to hate him and loudly lamented their
loss, extolled him.

6. *fraught*] freight, cargo.

7. *Candy*] the island of Crete, at that time called Candia.

8. *desperate . . . state*] reckless of disgrace and oblivious of his rank.

DUKE.   Notable pirate! thou salt-water thief!
　　　　What foolish boldness brought thee to their mercies,
　　　　Whom thou, in terms so bloody and so dear,
　　　　Hast made thine enemies?
ANT.　　　　　　　　　　　　Orsino, noble sir,
　　　　Be pleased that I shake off these names you give me:
　　　　Antonio never yet was thief or pirate,
　　　　Though I confess, on base and ground enough,
　　　　Orsino's enemy. A witchcraft drew me hither:
　　　　That most ingrateful boy there by your side,
　　　　From the rude sea's enraged and foamy mouth
　　　　Did I redeem; a wreck past hope he was:
　　　　His life I gave him and did thereto add
　　　　My love, without retention or restraint,
　　　　All his in dedication; for his sake
　　　　Did I expose myself, pure⁹ for his love,
　　　　Into the danger of this adverse town;
　　　　Drew to defend him when he was beset:
　　　　Where being apprehended, his false cunning,
　　　　Not meaning to partake with me in danger,
　　　　Taught him to face me out of his acquaintance,¹⁰
　　　　And grew a twenty years removed thing
　　　　While one would wink; denied me mine own purse,
　　　　Which I had recommended to his use
　　　　Not half an hour before.
VIO.　　　　　　　　　　　How can this be?
DUKE.   When came he to this town?
ANT.   To-day, my lord; and for three months before,
　　　　No interim, not a minute's vacancy,
　　　　Both day and night did we keep company.

Enter OLIVIA *and* Attendants

DUKE.   Here comes the countess: now heaven walks on earth.
　　　　But for thee, fellow; fellow, thy words are madness:
　　　　Three months this youth hath tended upon me;
　　　　But more of that anon. Take him aside.
OLI.   What would my lord, but that he may not have,
　　　　Wherein Olivia may seem serviceable?

─────────────

9. *pure*] the adjective used adverbially, "purely," "solely."
10. *face me . . . acquaintance*] brazenly deny knowledge of me.

      Cesario, you do not keep promise with me.

VIO.   Madam!

DUKE.   Gracious Olivia,—

OLI.   What do you say, Cesario? Good my lord,—

VIO.   My lord would speak; my duty hushes me.

OLI.   If it be aught to the old tune, my lord,
      It is as fat and fulsome[11] to mine ear
      As howling after music.

DUKE.   Still so cruel?

OLI.   Still so constant, lord.

DUKE.   What, to perverseness? you uncivil lady,
      To whose ingrate and unauspicious altars
      My soul the faithfull'st offerings hath breathed out
      That e'er devotion tender'd! What shall I do?

OLI.   Even what it please my lord, that shall become him.

DUKE.   Why should I not, had I the heart to do it,
      Like to the Egyptian thief at point of death,
      Kill what I love?—[12]a savage jealousy
      That sometimes savours nobly. But hear me this:
      Since you to non-regardance cast my faith,
      And that I partly know the instrument
      That screws me from my true place in your favour,
      Live you the marble-breasted tyrant still;
      But this your minion, whom I know you love,
      And whom, by heaven I swear, I tender dearly,
      Him will I tear out of that cruel eye,
      Where he sits crowned in his master's spite.
      Come, boy, with me; my thoughts are ripe in mischief:
      I'll sacrifice the lamb that I do love,
      To spite a raven's heart within a dove.

VIO.   And I, most jocund, apt and willing,
      To do you rest, a thousand deaths would die.

OLI.   Where goes Cesario?

VIO.   After him I love
      More than I love these eyes, more than my life,
      More, by all mores, than e'er I shall love wife.

---

11. *fat and fulsome*] nauseous and cloying.

12. *the Egyptian thief . . . love?*] A reference to the story of Theagenes and Chariclea in Heliodorus, *Æthiopica* (translated by Thomas Underdowne, 1569), where Thyamis, an Egyptian thief, slays a captive whom he mistakes for the object of his affection, in the fear that he is about to be robbed of her.

   If I do feign, you witnesses above
   Punish my life for tainting of my love!
OLI. Ay me, detested! how am I beguiled!
VIO. Who does beguile you? who does do you wrong?
OLI. Hast thou forgot thyself? is it so long?
   Call forth the holy father.
DUKE.   Come, away!
OLI. Whither, my lord? Cesario, husband, stay.
DUKE. Husband!
OLI.   Ay, husband: can he that deny?
DUKE. Her husband, sirrah!
VIO.   No, my lord, not I.
OLI. Alas, it is the baseness of thy fear
   That makes thee strangle thy propriety:[13]
   Fear not, Cesario; take thy fortunes up;
   Be that thou know'st thou art, and then thou art
   As great as that thou fear'st.

Enter Priest

        O, welcome, father!
   Father, I charge thee, by thy reverence,
   Here to unfold, though lately we intended
   To keep in darkness what occasion now
   Reveals before 't is ripe, what thou dost know
   Hath newly pass'd between this youth and me.
PRIEST. A contract of eternal bond of love,[14]
   Confirm'd by mutual joinder of your hands,
   Attested by the holy close of lips,
   Strengthen'd by interchangement of your rings;
   And all the ceremony of this compact
   Seal'd in my function,[15] by my testimony:
   Since when, my watch hath told me, toward my grave
   I have travell'd but two hours.
DUKE. O thou dissembling cub! what wilt thou be
   When time hath sow'd a grizzle on thy case?[16]
   Or will not else thy craft so quickly grow,

---

13. *propriety*] identity or individuality.
14. *A contract . . . love*] the ordinary ceremony of a betrothal, which preceeded the marriage rite.
15. *function*] office as chaplain to Olivia.
16. *a grizzle on thy case*] a touch of grey on thy skin.

That thine own trip shall be thine overthrow?
Farewell, and take her; but direct thy feet
Where thou and I henceforth may never meet.

VIO.　My lord, I do protest—

OLI.　　　　　　　　　　O, do not swear!
Hold little faith, though thou hast too much fear.

Enter SIR ANDREW

SIR AND.　For the love of God, a surgeon! Send one presently to Sir
Toby.

OLI.　What's the matter?

SIR AND.　He has broke my head across and has given Sir Toby a
bloody coxcomb too: for the love of God, your help! I had rather
than forty pound I were at home.

OLI.　Who has done this, Sir Andrew?

SIR AND.　The count's gentleman, one Cesario: we took him for a
coward, but he's the very devil incardinate.

DUKE.　My gentleman, Cesario?

SIR AND.　'Od's lifelings, here he is! You broke my head for nothing;
and that that I did, I was set on to do 't by Sir Toby.

VIO.　Why do you speak to me? I never hurt you:
You drew your sword upon me without cause;
But I bespake you fair, and hurt you not.

SIR AND.　If a bloody coxcomb be a hurt, you have hurt me: I think
you set nothing by a bloody coxcomb.

Enter SIR TOBY *and* Clown

Here comes Sir Toby halting; you shall hear more: but if he had
not been in drink, he would have tickled you othergates[17] than he
did.

DUKE.　How now, gentleman! how is 't with you?

SIR TO.　That's all one: has hurt me, and there 's the end on 't. Sot,
didst see Dick surgeon, sot?

CLO.　O, he 's drunk, Sir Toby, an hour agone; his eyes were set at
eight i' the morning.

SIR TO.　Then he 's a rogue, and a passy measures pavin:[18] I hate a
drunken rogue.

---

17. *othergates*] Sir Andrew's word for otherwise, in another manner.
18. *passy measures pavin*] "Pavin" is the name of a stately dance, and "passy measures" is
a corruption of "passamezzo," a slow and solemn step which formed chief part of the
"pavin."

OLI. Away with him! Who hath made this havoc with them?

SIR AND. I 'll help you, Sir Toby, because we 'll be dressed together.

SIR TO. Will you help? an ass-head and a coxcomb and a knave, a thin-faced knave, a gull!

OLI. Get him to bed, and let his hurt be look'd to.

[*Exeunt* Clown, FABIAN, SIR TOBY, *and* SIR ANDREW.]

Enter SEBASTIAN

SEB. I am sorry, madam, I have hurt your kinsman;
But, had it been the brother of my blood,
I must have done no less with wit and safety.
You throw a strange regard[19] upon me, and by that
I do perceive it hath offended you:
Pardon me, sweet one, even for the vows
We made each other but so late ago.

DUKE. One face, one voice, one habit, and two persons,
A natural perspective,[20] that is and is not!

SEB. Antonio, O my dear Antonio!
How have the hours rack'd and tortured me,
Since I have lost thee!

ANT. Sebastian are you?

SEB.   Fear'st thou that, Antonio?

ANT. How have you made division of yourself?
An apple, cleft in two, is not more twin
Than these two creatures. Which is Sebastian?

OLI. Most wonderful!

SEB. Do I stand there? I never had a brother;
Nor can there be that deity in my nature,
Of here and every where. I had a sister,
Whom the blind waves and surges have devour'd.
Of charity, what kin are you to me?
What countryman? what name? what parentage?

VIO. Of Messaline: Sebastian was my father;
Such a Sebastian was my brother too,
So went he suited[21] to his watery tomb:
If spirits can assume both form and suit,
You come to fright us.

---

19. *regard*] look.

20. *perspective*] an ingeniously contrived glass, which was capable of producing the optical delusion of making one person look like two.

21. *suited*] in such a suit of clothes.

SEB.   A spirit I am indeed;
    But am in that dimension grossly clad
    Which from the womb I did participate.
    Were you a woman, as the rest goes even,
    I should my tears let fall upon your cheek,
    And say, "Thrice-welcome, drowned Viola!"

VIO.   My father had a mole upon his brow.

SEB.   And so had mine.

VIO.   And died that day when Viola from her birth
    Had number'd thirteen years.

SEB.   O, that record is lively in my soul!
    He finished indeed his mortal act
    That day that made my sister thirteen years.

VIO.   If nothing lets[22] to make us happy both
    But this my masculine usurp'd attire,
    Do not embrace me till each circumstance
    Of place, time, fortune, do cohere and jump
    That I am Viola: which to confirm,
    I'll bring you to a captain in this town,
    Where lie my maiden weeds; by whose gentle help
    I was preserved to serve this noble count.
    All the occurrence of my fortune since
    Hath been between this lady and this lord.

SEB.   [To OLIVIA] So comes it, lady, you have been mistook:
    But nature to her bias drew in that.
    You would have been contracted to a maid;
    Nor are you therein, by my life, deceived,
    You are betroth'd both to a maid and man.

DUKE.   Be not amazed; right noble is his blood.
    If this be so, as yet the glass seems true,
    I shall have share in this most happy wreck.
    [To VIOLA] Boy, thou hast said to me a thousand times
    Thou never shouldst love woman like to me.

VIO.   And all those sayings will I over-swear;
    And all those swearings keep as true in soul
    As doth that orbed continent the fire
    That severs day from night.

DUKE.   Give me thy hand;
    And let me see thee in thy woman's weeds.

---

22. *lets*] prevents.

Vio.   The captain that did bring me first on shore
       Hath my maid's garments: he upon some action
       Is now in durance, at Malvolio's suit,
       A gentleman, and follower of my lady's.
Oli.   He shall enlarge him: fetch Malvolio hither:
       And yet, alas, now I remember me,
       They say, poor gentleman, he 's much distract.

Re-enter Clown *with a letter, and* Fabian

       A most extracting frenzy of mine own
       From my remembrance clearly banish'd his.
       How does he, sirrah?
Clo.   Truly, madam, he holds Belzebub at the stave's end as well as a
       man in his case may do: has here writ a letter to you; I should have
       given 't you to-day morning, but as a madman's epistles are no
       gospels, so it skills not much when they are delivered.
Oli.   Open 't, and read it.
Clo.   Look then to be well edified when the fool delivers the mad-
       man. [*Reads*] By the Lord, madam,—
Oli.   How now! art thou mad?
Clo.   No, madam, I do but read madness: an your ladyship will have
       it as it ought to be, you must allow Vox.[23]
Oli.   Prithee, read i' thy right wits.
Clo.   So I do, madonna; but to read his right wits is to read thus:
       therefore perpend,[24] my princess, and give ear.
Oli.   Read it you, sirrah.   [*To* Fabian.]
Fab.   [*Reads*] By the Lord, madam, you wrong me, and the world shall know
       it: though you have put me into darkness and given your drunken cousin
       rule over me, yet have I the benefit of my senses as well as your ladyship.
       I have your own letter that induced me to the semblance I put on; with
       the which I doubt not but to do myself much right, or you much shame.
       Think of me as you please. I leave my duty a little unthought of, and
       speak out of my injury.

                                       The madly-used Malvolio.
Oli.   Did he write this?
Clo.   Ay, madam.
Duke. This savours not much of distraction.
Oli.   See him deliver'd, Fabian; bring him hither.   [*Exit* Fabian.]
       My lord, so please you, these things further thought on,

---

23. *allow Vox*] allow me the use of my voice.
24. *perpend*] consider.

To think me as well a sister as a wife,
One day shall crown the alliance on 't, so please you,
Here at my house and at my proper cost.

DUKE.   Madam, I am most apt to embrace your offer.
[*To* VIOLA] Your master quits you; and for your service done him,
So much against the mettle of your sex,
So far beneath your soft and tender breeding,
And since you call'd me master for so long,
Here is my hand: you shall from this time be
Your master's mistress.

OLI.   A sister! you are she.

Re-enter FABIAN, *with* MALVOLIO

DUKE.   Is this the madman?

OLI.   Ay, my lord, this same.
How now, Malvolio!

MAL.   Madam, you have done me wrong,
Notorious wrong.

OLI.   Have I, Malvolio? no.

MAL.   Lady, you have. Pray you, peruse that letter.
You must not now deny it is your hand:
Write from it,²⁵ if you can, in hand or phrase;
Or say 't is not your seal, not your invention:
You can say none of this: well, grant it then
And tell me, in the modesty of honour,
Why you have given me such clear lights of favour,
Bade me come smiling and cross-garter'd to you,
To put on yellow stockings and to frown
Upon Sir Toby and the lighter people;
And, acting this in an obedient hope,
Why have you suffer'd me to be imprison'd,
Kept in a dark house, visited by the priest,
And made the most notorious geck²⁶ and gull
That e'er invention play'd on? tell my why.

OLI.   Alas, Malvolio, this is not my writing,
Though, I confess, much like the character:
But out of question 't is Maria's hand.
And now I do bethink me, it was she

---

25. *Write from it*] Write differently from it.
26. *geck*] dupe.

First told me thou wast mad; then camest in smiling,
And in such forms which here were presupposed
Upon thee in the letter. Prithee, be content:
This practice hath most shrewdly pass'd upon thee;
But when we know the grounds and authors of it,
Thou shalt be both the plaintiff and the judge
Of thine own cause.

FAB.   Good madam, hear me speak,
And let no quarrel nor no brawl to come
Taint the condition of this present hour,
Which I have wonder'd at. In hope it shall not,
Most freely I confess, myself and Toby
Set this device against Malvolio here,
Upon some stubborn and uncourteous parts
We had conceived against him: Maria writ
The letter at Sir Toby's great importance;[27]
In recompense whereof he hath married her.
How with a sportful malice it was follow'd
May rather pluck on laughter than revenge;
If that the injuries be justly weigh'd
That have on both sides pass'd.

OLI.   Alas, poor fool, how have they baffled thee!

CLO.   Why, "some are born great, some achieve greatness, and some
have greatness thrown upon them." I was one, sir, in this inter-
lude; one Sir Topas, sir; but that's all one. "By the Lord, fool, I am
not mad." But do you remember? "Madam, why laugh you at such
a barren rascal? an you smile not, he's gagged": and thus the
whirligig of time brings in his revenges.

MAL.   I'll be revenged on the whole pack of you.   [*Exit.*]

OLI.   He hath been most notoriously abused.

DUKE.   Pursue him, and entreat him to a peace:
He hath not told us of the captain yet:
When that is known, and golden time convents,[28]
A solemn combination shall be made
Of our dear souls. Meantime, sweet sister,
We will not part from hence. Cesario, come;
For so you shall be, while you are a man;
But when in other habits you are seen,

---

27. *importance*] insistent request.
28. *convents*] suits.

Orsino's mistress and his fancy's queen.

[*Exeunt all, except* Clown.]

CLO. [*Sings*]

> When that I was and a little tiny boy,
>   With hey, ho, the wind and the rain,
> A foolish thing was but a toy,
>   For the rain it raineth every day.
>
> But when I came to man's estate,
>   With hey, ho, &c.
> 'Gainst knaves and thieves men shut their gate,
>   For the rain, &c.
>
> But when I came, alas! to wive,
>   With hey, ho, &c.
> By swaggering could I never thrive,
>   For the rain, &c.
>
> But when I came unto my beds,
>   With hey, ho, &c.
> With toss-pots still had drunken heads,
>   For the rain, &c.
>
> A great while ago the world begun,
>   With hey, ho, &c.
> But that's all one, our play is done,
>   And we 'll strive to please you every day.   [*Exit.*]